MURDER ON THE GENEVA EXPRESS

A MAC AND MILLIE MYSTERY

JB MICHAELS

HARRISONANDJAMESPUBLISHING.COM

For Aunt Debbie

MURDER ON THE GENEVA EXPRESS

A Mac and Millie Mystery

BY

JB Michaels

CHAPTER ONE

Peter Rickman's time grew short. His good time. The alcohol he so effortlessly imbibed in celebration of his brother's last night as a bachelor, had begun to fade. His buzz that once numbed his pain would soon become the source of his pain. He welcomed weekend hangovers; it made things easier for him. He could just cower away in his state of misery or drink more to sustain the intoxication for a few hours, if not for the whole of the next day and night.

He pulled a flask from his jacket pocket and guzzled the last third of scotch from his personal liquor collection. He put the flask back into his pocket and lifted his head, sweeping his gaze around the second deck of the commuter train. He could focus on the steel grey of the luggage/bag rack. He'd taken the train a grand total of twelve times this week: to and from downtown Chicago on his way to his 1.5-million-dollar mansion near the famed Third Street of Geneva, Illinois. His thirteenth trip was for his brother's bachelor party; a weekend binge with an uproarious axe throwing contest, a subsequent liquid dinner with plentiful appetizers at a fancy Greek restaurant, and then a private, exotic dance at Peter's multi-purpose downtown condo. He should have crashed there last night but he felt the need to be home and closer to his wife.

Danny Rickman drooled on his shoulder. He felt the warmth of his little brother's slobbery secretion soak through his shirt on his left shoulder. The train rumbled and began to slow for arrival at Third Street Station. Peter looked to his right shoulder to examine another trickle of warm liquid. It certainly was not possible for his brother to drool so much that it dripped down both his shoulders. No, this liquid was warm and crimson. A drip here and a spot there gave way to a full-grown torrent of blood gushing from what was no doubt his head.

Peter attempted one last look at his little brother

before his vision blurred and the interior of the train car swirled and swirled followed by darkness.

DANNY WOKE from his drunken slumber as the train slowed then stopped and his head support for his nap disappeared. His brother had fallen onto the walkway in a heap; his body blocked people from exiting the train car.

"Peter, dude, we are so drunk—oh shit. We gotta get off the train. Come on man. Peter."

It took a few seconds for Danny to realize that his brother's head lay in a pool of blood. A man with a cane in his hand kneeled near his head.

"What the fuck, man? Did you... did you hit my brother?" Danny stammered.

"No, I just saw him pass out and came over to help." The man with the cane attempted an explanation. "Honestly, I did not..."

"Pete. Pete! No man! No!" Danny fell to his knees and cradled his brother's head, holding his lifeless body against him. The train floor was filthy and stained with his brother's blood.

The rest of the bachelor party woke from their drunken slumber and found them within moments.

Six men all in their late twenties crowded around Peter and the man with the cane.

"I can explain, gentlemen." The man with the cane, the accused attacker, said. "I saw Pete fall to the ground and I came over to help him. I used to be a cop. It's instinctual for me to want to help in situations like this. Don't do anything stupid. We don't need any other bad things happening on this train."

The group of bachelors circled around the man with the cane, ready to pound him. Their inebriation only fueled their rage.

"How the fuck else did the side of my brother's head just burst open?!" Danny gently put his brother's head back down.

Word traveled fast. The crowding of the train car and the screaming accusations alerted the train conductor. He walked through the double doors from the front of the commuter train.

"Gentlemen, please, can we clear the area? What happened here? Do I need to call an ambulance or the cops? What's happening?" The blue uniformed conductor tipped his train cap upward and spoke into a handheld walkie talkie. He'd seen Pete's body. "Don't move the train. Call in a delay."

A voice burst over the receiver confirming the train delay.

"Gentlemen, please." The burly black train conductor pushed three of Danny's friends to the side. The man with the cane immediately pushed his way back towards the train conductor, but not before Danny grabbed his leg and yanked him backward.

The man with the cane fell into the arms of the conductor. The conductor caught him and tried to pull him back from the mob: men punched his ribs and the side of his head, and Danny squeezed his testicles hard. Very, very hard.

The man with the cane screamed.

"Enough!" The conductor yelled but was then overtaken by Danny's friends. He fell in between the blood orange seating and to the narrow train floor. The man with the cane fell with him. And then it all seemed to happen at once: Danny let go of the man's crotch. The train conductor, in a fit of rage, threw the man with the cane towards the seats on his left. The man with the cane scrambled over the top of the seats to reach the exit of the train car.

Danny pulled himself up from the floor. The train conductor was still battling his friends and their ridiculous scrum stopped him from pursuing the man who killed his brother. He watched the man with the cane flee. He had to let him go.

He knelt next to his brother and lifted his head

back into his lap. He heard the wail of police and ambulance sirens in the distance. Danny was to be married this weekend and his best man lay dead in his arms.

CHAPTER

TWO

"Whoa. Did you see that register?"

"Um, yeah."

"Shut up. You lied. You didn't see it did you?"

"I definitely didn't see it. Sorry, I'm too busy playing on this new app. What was it?"

"I think we need to call this one in."

"What do you mean call it in? Why? What happens out here?"

"Nothing usually, but something crazy just happened. Check the register on what this alarm is." Raj showed his partner the alarm code: a crimson skull barred behind a traditional, circular prohibited sign.

"No way." Matt dropped his phone onto the floor.

"Yes. This alarm registered. The regs just called it in too. Police and emergency vehicles are headed to the scene. Something bad happened—something *really* bad happened. We need to call her in."

"Call in Constable Greene now? Are you sure that we can do that? Is she back yet from her last assignment? Isn't she too high up?" Matt shook his head and fumbled with the work phone, an old analog landline that no one had touched for years.

"Just do it now! Looks like someone fled the scene too and is hobbling down Third Street as we speak." Raj looked through a mirror that showed a man with a cane hopping down Third towards the Tiny Wanderer.

Constable Greene put her jacket on the hanger and then rubbed her wand down the front of it to smooth out any wrinkles—and get rid of any excess magic that could still be clinging to it. She rubbed the front of the jacket in a meticulous, yet efficient, manner and then turned to the back and did the same thing. No need for any middle of the night jolts from the absorption power this piece of magic armor held within it. She loved this black leather jacket; it was her favorite jacket and her blanket of security. It only warmed her during very short seasonal times of the year, so it wasn't practical from the regular world's perspective. How wrong they were: it had practically saved her life many times.

The proper clothes do make the woman. The professional; the seriousness with which she carried herself and her position. Tonight, she felt she might be able to relax after the Dekalb assignment was over except for filing the last paperwork. She put her wand down and walked the jacket to the closet. As she reached to place the hanger on the rod, the buzzing of her phone sounded from the jacket's interior pocket and halted her movement.

She sighed. She fished the phone from her pocket.

The Geneva station: a usually quiet station except for some excessive essence of hummingbird sales a couple years back. Nothing ever happened there from the magical world's perspective, but if did, the Geneva local constabulary usually kept it in house. It never reached any of the higher ranks like her.

Greene rolled her eyes.

The phone kept buzzing.

She sighed again and then answered, "This is Constable Greene."

"We have an alarm. Protocol is to reach out to you

on this one, ma'am." The voice on the other end of the line trembled. *Inexperienced.*

"Slow down. Breathe." Constable Greene pulled her jacket off of the hanger. She looked out the window to the east and the view of dawn's dim light over Lake Michigan; then to the south and the sparkling skyline of the city of Chicago. She just wanted to be home, to take a bath, and go to bed.

The voice on the end of the line sounded confused. "You really want me to—"

"Yes, take a deep breath and give me more details on the alarm."

An audible breath sounded through the receiver.

And then silence—for too long.

"You can breathe now." Constable Greene shook her head.

"Yes, ma'am, that was a great tip by the way. Sorry. Sorry, it's been so long since—"

She closed her eyes to control her temper. "The alarm Constable. Please."

"A Crimson Skull. Legit; a crimson skull flashed in our mirror here. And we have a runner. Someone who fled the scene: a man hobbling with a cane. Our owls followed him into an old retail mansion called the Tiny Wanderer. From what we can tell, he is still inside the mansion."

"Good. I will be there shortly. Keep the owls perched in the trees above the Wanderer. Don't lose him. Do we have ID on this person?"

"Yes. Man is named Mac O'Malley, former reg police officer."

CHAPTER
THREE

Mac O'Malley holed up in the newly renovated Atrium café. His heart beat much harder than normal, not only from moving fast down Third to The Tiny Wanderer, but also from the fear of a situation he'd never found himself in before: the prime suspect in a murder and with the possible murder weapon in his hand. He recounted the events in his head. He paced the floor without the use of his cane; he examined it with the flashlight from his phone. Were there any markers on it to indicate he *did* strike the man in the head with the cane? There was a lot of blood. There had been a ton spewing from the side of the man's head.

Mac remembered he'd nodded off on the train. He awoke to a man yelling for someone to wake up. He'd quickly sprung into action to help when the man who screamed—but it turned out to be the vic's brother. He'd accused Mac of killing his brother with a devastating blow to the side of his head, using the cane Mac examined as the weapon. The cane was a replica of a prop in one of Mac's favorite films, *The Wolfman*. As much as Mac trusted what he saw, and tried to will it from his mind, the more prevalent the dark reality set in. The handle of the cane resembled the head of the wolf and was covered in bloodstains. Mac had seen his fair share of murder weapons. This cane, *his* cane, was used to murder a man on the Geneva Express?

The pit in his stomach grew larger. Someone on the train had grabbed his cane and then was powerful enough to use it to bludgeon a man in the head with one powerful blow and kill him. Or could something else have happened? Maybe he hit his head earlier which caused some bleeding from his ear; maybe it got worse over time and he was too drunk to notice.

No. Someone in his party would have noticed.

Mac shook his head and forced in a deep breath. The Atrium Café was dark and newly renovated. It was refreshed to look like the original that had been ravaged by an awful storm a few months ago. It normally eased his mind but tonight it didn't. He sat on a wrought iron chair; he needed to gather his thoughts. He needed to just stroll back to the scene and talk to his brother, Vince, and explain exactly what happened. Not many other plausible suspects had the luxury of having their brother on the force—and probably the responding detective on a fresh crime scene. He could just go back and explain that he was afraid of getting beat down by a group of drunk bachelors and that he responded to a slumped man who, upon examination, happened to be hemorrhaging blood from the side of his head.

Simple.

Mac stood in the dark Atrium Café. He activated his phone's flashlight once more to find his way out, but before leaving, he looked down at his cane once more. The snarled snout and piercing eyes of the werewolf stared back at him. A chill managed to raise the hair on the back of his neck and his arms.

"Snap out of it, Mac." Mac drove the cane into the tile floor and made his way forward to the Fulton Street exit.

He stopped.

He wasn't sure if this was the right move. He needed some guidance. Sometimes, tough situations required consulting with his best partner, Millie.

"Sorry it's so late, Millie, but I need to talk to

someone about this." He mumbled as he dialed her number.

The phone rang and rang.

"Mac. It's 4:10 in the morning. What's happening? You okay?" Millie asked.

"Usually, I give a flippant answer: yes. But no. I am definitely not okay. In the next few hours—or sooner—I might be officially wanted for murder."

CHAPTER
FOUR

Millie was rattled when she answered the phone with a flourish. Mac startled her from a deep sleep. Why on earth was he calling this late? Or, one could make the argument, this early?

"Mac, I need you to slow down. Why are you suddenly a murder suspect in the middle of the night?"

"I was downtown last night...or tonight, I guess. I took the train and, on the way back, a guy collapsed on the train. Blood was spewing out of the side of his head—"

"Wait. Slow it down. Where are you right now? Are you with Vince? Did you call your brother?" Millie stood up and started pulling her pajama pants down.

"I didn't call him. I ran from the scene as fast as I could because an angry group of bachelor party drunks were gonna kill me. They think I killed their friend with my cane!"

Millie heard a tone. She pulled the phone away from her ear and looked at the notification.

EMERGENCY-USE OF FORBIDDEN MAGIC IN GENEVA IL AREA. SHELTER-IN-PLACE UNTIL FURTHER NOTICE

"Mac, where are you right now?" I'll come and get you."

"The café at the Tiny Wanderer. Edith gave me a key after the whole Raftery's Ghost debacle."

"I will be right there. Hang tight."

"Okay. Love you. See you soon."

"Love you too. I'll be right there. Stay put and don't get all excited about a hunch or something and move." Millie ended the call and pulled on a pair of ripped jeans from her bedroom floor.

She couldn't remember the last time she saw a Dark Magic alert. And the Constabulary sends this alert the same night Mac thinks he'll be accused of murder. What the hell was he doing in downtown Chicago anyway? By himself and on the train? The wedding was a month away and he'd been acting strange lately. Was he getting cold feet? He *had* been a bachelor for a long time. Was marriage something he really wanted?

Millie zipped up a hoodie, pushed her feet into her shoes, and walked out the door. She needed to get Mac to safety. She hadn't wanted to alarm him even more, but the use of forbidden magic meant that someone was either tortured or killed. The only other time she'd heard of dark magic being used was when she was in the sixth grade. A group of eighth graders used a Ouija board and ended up ripping Maria D'anoto's hair from her scalp. The group of teens accidentally used the dark magic, no actual malice intended, but messing with anything remotely related to dark magic had a cost. It was always nasty—and people always paid.

She started the car and screeched away from her apartment complex. She was worried about Mac. Dark Magic or not, he needed her help.

CHAPTER
FIVE

"As I said before, 5'11, brown hair, blue eyes, late 30s or so. Walked with a cane—the same he used to kill my fucking brother!"

"Sir, we can't jump to any conclusions. Did you see him hit your brother in the head with his cane?" Vince shook his head. The guy was visibly upset and the stench of alcohol assaulted his olfactory nerves to the point his eyes started to water.

The brother of the deceased screamed, "He killed my brother, man!"

"You don't know that!" Vince yelled.

"Officer O'Malley, why don't you let me handle this?" His reliable, young partner Officer Jackson urged him to take a breather with a firm clap of his hand against Vince's shoulder.

"Shit. You're right." Vince walked over to the dead body in the middle of the commuter train walkway. He saw the large contusion on the side of the head. Vince winced and massaged the bridge of his nose in a fast, aggressive manner. He was stressed and worried because the possible perpetrator and prime suspect matched the description of his brother and hero cop, Mac O'Malley.

"Mac, were you on this train?" He whispered to himself. Vince heard Jackson interview the witnesses and had resisted the urge to listen closely. He almost did not want to know how many others would describe the same, exact person; that would make it true. Why would Mac kill Peter Rickman on a commuter train in the middle of the night? Vince looked toward the double exit door of the train car. He would just walk outside, call his brother, and everything would be fine. Mac was sleeping in his bed. There were plenty of other assholes in their late 30s with canes…who rode commuter trains.

Outside on the train platform, Mac's silver-haired, older brother dialed the familiar number. The phone rang and rang.

"Come on you idiot, answer the damn phone!" Vince paced. The paramedics were prepping the gurney to remove the body. Vince moved out of the way.

"Pick up you moron!" He walked away from the train.

A beep resounded in his ear. Call waiting.

His Sergeant.

"Shit." Vince switched to his superior's call.

"Vincey, yeah, I'm sure you figured out why I am calling."

"Big fucking surprise! I'm off the case!"

"Vincey, don't make this any worse than it already is. My best detective can't be on the case. The witnesses all describe his brother. There's no denying it. You try gettin' a hold of him?"

"Ah, shit! I get it. I just tried calling...he isn't answering."

"Vince, now just go home to the wife and kids. Okay? Just take a couple days off."

"Yeah, yeah, yeah." Vince hung up the phone; he wanted to throw it 300 yards away. Jackson would have to take this one. Vince knew he needed to calm down, gather his thoughts, and find his brother. He sure as hell wasn't off the case, not in his mind. Officially yes. Unofficially, hell no.

"Where are you little brother?"

CHAPTER
SIX

Millie drove through the dark streets of Geneva. Her heart raced; she didn't even realize how quickly she accelerated over the 30mph speed limit. Still, most cops would be at the train station responding to the murder scene. She sped down Fulton and up to the dimly lit Tiny Wanderer, the sprawling Italianate retail mansion and current hiding place of Mac O'Malley.

She was particularly creeped out by the home addition that served as a storage room. The upstairs was well documented in the ghost log kept current by the staff of the Tiny Wanderer, something she experienced firsthand just a few months ago. Lore circled around bouncing balls, children crying, and cold spells and some said the addition was more haunted than the original mansion. The yellow ambient light of the Third Street lamps cast just enough light to give the building an eerie, ominous appearance.

Millie pulled into the parking spot right in front of the awning-covered side entrance. Her nerves continued to rattle and she bobbled her phone when she tried to call Mac. Sucking in a sharp breath to settle herself, she dialed and held the phone to her ear.

Mac's phone rang and rang.

She pulled her phone away and saw a text message.

Someone is looking for me in here. - Mac.

A mysterious person had reached the Wanderer before her. Millie secured her wand and exited her Nissan. Upon her exit, she looked for other cars, but hers was the only vehicle on this side of Fulton. She heard the hoot of several owls above her.

The owls.

Oh shit. Someone else with magical powers was near and had used the owls to track down Mac. It could be the Dark Magic user! Millie walked under the once-yellow-now-light-blue awning of the Fulton Street entrance. The darkness wouldn't help anyone.

She spoke the words to her wand, "Fireflies."

A singular spark spurted from the tip of her wand. Her spell failed. Millie looked up at the owls and realized that someone had also cast a restrictive charm on the area. It could have been the Constabulary, cast to prevent the use of forbidden magic...but it could have been the person looking for Mac in the Wanderer.

The Fulton Street door was ajar, and she could see through the glass panes next to the door. She still had her phone flashlight, but she thought better of it: fireflies and light might draw unwanted attention to her.

Her phone vibrated.

Making a run for it. Out the Fulton door. - Mac

Millie messaged back, **Okay. I will get the car ready!**

Millie snatched the keys from her pocket and ran to the car. As the engine hummed to life, Mac burst through the door; he was hobbling, but moving fast. Millie leaned to the passenger door and pushed it open for him.

Mac collapsed into the car. He made sure his cane cleared the threshold of the door and said, "Floor it!"

Millie pulled away quickly and headed away from Third Street. She was certain the owls gave chase and were tracking them. She had to find a way to lose them. "Shit. Mac, we have multiple issues. Owls are chasing us, too. I think we have both the Constabulary *and* the cops after you!"

"Owls, you said... like, actual owls? Do they transform into people or something?"

"No, they are used for surveillance and tracking—especially at night. We're in big trouble and have to figure out a way to ditch them."

"Why don't we just talk to the Constabulary? Why would they be hunting me down?"

"Someone used Dark Magic in Geneva tonight and there is a restrictive charm in place to stop all magic users. The Constabulary doesn't mess around with Dark Magic use; they will detain you and possibly jail you for an indefinite length of time. The Constabulary plays by very different rules than regular human justice systems."

"They will clearly know that I'm not a magic user."

"Yes, but I am, and I have been seen aiding you. They know you just ran from the scene of a crime and tracked you the whole way. I'm basically a suspect too," Millie said.

"Okay, so now we are both wanted."

"Did you get a look at the person who hunted for you in the Wanderer? Did they identify themselves in any way?"

"No, it was one person who used a big flashlight. It helped me track them and stay out of their way. Also, the Wanderer itself helped me, as whoever it was must have gotten lost and got turned around—which allowed me to get from the café to the exit off Fulton. They went upstairs and I bolted."

"We should head to 272. My mom might be able to help us lose the owls and hide us for now."

"Why don't we just call them first? We don't want to lead the owls to your parents. Let's stay mobile." Mac put his hand on Millie's knee.

"Good point. Sorry, I am so flustered by this whole situation."

CHAPTER
SEVEN

Constable Greene aimed her flashlight at some old mannequins that looked too chipped and old to be stored in a working retail shop. Her search inside the strange building failed.

The owls were certainly monitoring the situation.

She felt her phone buzz. She answered, "What's happening? I'm coming up empty here."

"The owls have moved and we think our suspect may have left the premises. They are following someone else, and it looks like they're in a car. The owls are flying in a high-altitude position."

"Let me know when they stop. I'm going to the crime scene." The Constable sighed and ended the call before her junior constable could respond.

She would get this suspect no matter what; no matter the cost. The use of Dark Magic could tip the fragile peace off the ledge and into a full-blown, cultist uprising. The last time events like this happened was in the early 90s. She had a long history of no new incidents under her watch and tonight that could all end. Greene needed to keep the record intact. Nothing would disturb the peace under her purview.

Nothing.

Constable Greene followed the floor and retraced her steps. She didn't want to use any magic, as the area had been locked down from any magical use. She found her way back to the stairwell. The random cold spots throughout the retail mansion convinced her of some paranormal presence. She wasn't spooked by it, but certainly preferred to be elsewhere.

Preferably, Third Street Station.

She wound her way back to the Candy section, through the wine room, and then out a side door, which she easily unlocked with a trusty lock pick. The trusting world of Geneva certainly gave her pause; it was hard to believe that places with just a single door lock still existed—not robust, high-tech security systems. Of course, maybe the ghostly presence was enough to keep criminals away.

She walked out of the Tiny Wanderer and reached

into her wallet for her badge. It was enchanted and could transform for any situation she needed access to: in this case, she could use a federal badge. The FBI badge usually worked in cases like this, but a Metro Train police badge might work better. It was a small force and probably hadn't responded to the incident yet. She still had time.

The idyllic strip of Geneva, Third Street, was lit up by emergency vehicles and full-scale crime scene investigators. No Metro police cars yet. She approached Third Street station, which sat next to a well-built, limestone condo building. *Must cost a fortune to have a unit there.*

The train car doors were open and there were still a few police officers huddled around talking. She would love to see the victim, but she figured the body was removed at this point and sent to the medical examiner. She could still benefit from inspecting the crime scene, though.

She crouched under the yellow tape without having to identify herself. Her leather jacket, jeans, and long raven hair certainly wasn't a uniform and she really shouldn't have made it this far. No one stopped her.

She entered the train car and looked to a marked spot and a large pool of blood. She scanned the maroon seats next to the bloodied floor and noticed a lot of blood on part of the seat cushion closest to the aisle. It was clear to her what happened: the victim started bleeding profusely while he sat on the seat and then fell into the aisle. She looked to the windows and surrounding area around for additional blood spatter.

No spots.

No spray.

Hear-No-Evil dark magic. It was a nasty potion developed by a militant group of witches and wizards to combat the Salem Witch Hunts in the 1690s. Since spectral evidence was used to murder innocent magic users, spellbinders found a way to stop people from lying and reporting to religious authorities by decimating their ability to remember, see, hear, and communicate. The potion used for defense against witch hunts ultimately caused more hysteria. Damaging memories and rendering people deaf, mute, and blind is not a good use of magic. Ever.

This derangement of magic made into a potion could cause hemorrhages and death. Constable Greene felt she had a good idea what dark magic was used.

"Excuse me ma'am. You can't be in here!" A uniformed policeman yelled from the double doors of the train car entrance. "This is an active crime scene!"

"I was a passenger asleep in the upper deck in the middle rack. I know I'm not supposed to lay up there. So sorry. I am leaving now. I'm so sorry." Tears streamed down her face. She knew the rack didn't have any visibility from the lower deck and hoped they didn't do a thorough enough search. It was risky. But, based on how easy it was to cross the police tape, it might just work.

"We cleared the train an hour ago. We must have missed you. It's okay"

Constable Greene put on her best act as a bewildered civilian. "Again, I'm sorry."

She walked past the officer and stepped off the train. No harm. No foul.

CHAPTER EIGHT

Millie leaned out the driver's side window and tried to spot the owls overhead. There were two she could make out—one white and brown—and only because the lights on Route 38 helped her. Owls could fly for very long periods of time, even over vast bodies of water, for hundreds, if not, thousands of miles.

"Calling Mom now. How are we going to lose these damn owls?" Millie pulled her phone from the center console of the car and dialed Becca.

"Good morning. You never call this early. Is everything okay?" Becca sounded unusually calm due to the early morning hours. Pre-coffee most likely.

"We have problems, Mom. Mac and I are being tracked by Constabulary owls and we can't shake them." Millie heard the doorbell in the background followed by loud knocks.

"Oh dear, someone is pounding on our door. My gosh. What is happening? Hang on Millie."

Millie heard a shuffle and the door opened.

"Rebecca Paderson, Geneva PD. We just want to ask you a few questions. Mind if we come in?"

"I will call you back." Becca ended the call.

"Shit. GPD is at 272, probably trying to track you down—which could also mean they are trying to contact me, too, and see what I know." Mille shook her head. "We can't hide out anywhere here."

"We still have to lose these owls too, Millie." Mac sighed.

"Well, let's get out of Geneva completely. They can't block magic everywhere. We can head to a parking garage and try to lose them there." Millie stepped on the gas. The engine roared.

"Wouldn't they just circle around and wait until we came out again?" Mac asked.

"I think maybe we need to call Vince."

"Good point. Vince won't throw me in jail and they probably took him off the case as soon as the guys on train gave a description of me." Mac examined his phone. "He's already tried calling me."

"Okay, we'll head to the St. Charles parking garage on 2nd Avenue. We could have him meet us there."

"Hopefully he has some info for us. Something to help us so we can start our investigation to clear my name. Calling him now." Mac dialed his brother and put the phone on speaker.

"Mac! What the hell is going on? Please tell me you weren't on the train this morning?" Vince used an aggressive, loud tone.

"I was on the train, which is why I'm calling. I need your help; Millie and I need your help. We need to borrow your car and we need a lead."

"Whoa. Take it easy. Slow it down. Where are you headed?" Vince asked.

"St. Charles parking garage. 2nd Ave." Millie chimed in.

"Good morning, Millie, sorry my idiot brother got you in this mess. I'll meet you there; I'm leaving now. I have the minivan. Hope that's okay?"

"I hate minivans. Whatever." Mac shook his head.

"See you two soon." Vince ended the call.

CHAPTER NINE

The early morning sun from the east lit up River Road and thus Mac and Millie's route to St. Charles, north along the Fox River.

"Mac, stick your head out and see where the owls are."

"Still there and keeping pace with us. How do we know they won't just perch in trees around the parking garage and wait for us to exit? How do they even know to track me?"

"Just your description and owls have incredible eyesight. Period."

Mac shook his head. "Thought they only saw better at night?"

"False, I had a pet owl as a kid. They can see in the daylight just fine." Millie kept one hand on the wheel and fished her wand from her purse. "We should be clear of Geneva now."

She peered through the windshield and to her right: Oak Hill Cemetery and the border between Geneva and St. Charles. "Hope we are clear of the magic ban." Millie rolled her window down.

"Won't the Constabulary be able to trace this?" Mac asked.

"Bam! Pow!" Millie aimed her wand at the trees along River Road.

"That's the actual spell? What does that do?"

"Hopefully it worked. I will keep my eyes on the road." Millie left her wand on the dashboard and secured both hands on the wheel. "You tell me if it worked!"

"What am I looking for?" Mac rolled down his window and stuck his head out, looking up to the sky. The trees swayed. The leaves rustled. The trees began to shake. Loud screeches sounded in the air above; sudden swirls of dark matter spewed from the tree branches and the ground near the riverbank. It took Mac a second to realize how badass Millie's last spell was: she'd sent swarms of bats into the air to obscure and disrupt the vision and path of their aerial antagonists.

The owls were nowhere to be found. Millie drove further north along River Road.

"It worked! We lost them! That was incredible!"

"We aren't outta the woods yet. We have to ditch my car. I'm surprised we haven't been pulled over yet." Millie half-smiled. Her worry didn't wane.

"Coming up on St. Charles now." Mac pointed. They first saw a small, green pedestrian bridge, followed by the Route 64 bridge, and the majestic—and very haunted—Hotel Basil. The tan brick, century-old, hotel contrasted with the new buildings across the street, replete with restaurants, condos, and, of course, a Starbricks.

"The parking garage is just to the right up this hill. Let's hope Vince is already here." Millie drove up the hill and turned left into the middle level.

"What a crazy morning." Mac observed.

"Yes, and the day just started. I don't know, Mac. I don't have a good feeling about this one."

CHAPTER
TEN

"540 West Madison. Why are you giving me this address?" Mac examined the piece of paper his brother had given him.

"The vic's name is Peter Rickman. He was a bigshot at an investment firm downtown; that's the address. It's almost time for work. He obviously wouldn't be there today, but his staff still should be. Took the day off for the rehearsal dinner for his brother's wedding. The guy who ID'ed you as the prime suspect gave me some info before Jackson had me taken off the case," Vince answered.

Mac, Millie, and Vince stood in the lower level of the parking garage on 2nd street in downtown St. Charles. Vince handed the minivan keys to Mac. "The car is registered to Maggie so you should be okay driving it. See what you can find out about Rickman from his place of work. See if anyone would want to off this guy. I'll just take a cab back home."

"You know they have apps for that now. Nobody really uses cabs anymore." Mac shook his head. "Find anything else about the wound? What caused the bleeding?"

"I prefer cabs. Shut up. All we could determine at the scene was that it was a head wound. We won't know much else until after autopsy. Keep me updated with any updates you might find. I'll see what I can do from here." Vince started making his way to the stairwell in the corner of the parking garage.

"Thanks, Vincey. I really appreciate the help."

"Oh, I almost forgot. The bag on the passenger seat has a few burner phones. Use those. You can't use your own cellphones. You're a wanted man, brother. Don't worry, though, we will get you out of this."

Millie looked visibly upset. Her cheeks blushed. Her breath was shallow.

Mac let out a huge sigh. He took out his cellphone and powered it down, then put his hand out to Millie. She fished the phone from her purse and held the button to power it down and placed it in Mac's palm. He dropped the phones to the ground, raised his cane, and brought the wolf handle down on both screens rendering them inoperable.

She said, "Again, I just have a bad feeling about this one, Mac."

CONSTABLE GREENE WALKED down Rt. 25 next to the Fox River and examined the injured owls hopping around on the riverbank. The birds of prey dedicated and bred to serve the Constabulary were taken out masterfully by a capable magic user.

One owl had a batwing in its mouth. The other had a few feathers torn from the right wing.

"Do we have an ID on the car yet?" Constable Greene held the phone to her ear and put her other hand on her hip. She looked out to the Fox River's opposite bank. The morning light showed a large mansion with roman columns—it could be a good retirement home someday. If retirement were even an option for her; not from lack of planning, but from desire to stop working.

"Yes, belongs to Millie Paderson. She's a magic user. A capable witch. Was flagged a couple years ago for buying too much essence of hummingbird. Other than that, she is clean—but she earned the highest marks in the Academy. 'Proceed with caution' is what the system says. She's not wanted, but she is powerful." The junior constable said.

"I know her. We went to school together. She used bats to blind and obstruct the owls. They're injured, so send someone to pick them up asap. Why would someone who stays out of trouble be aiding a possible dark magic user? Do we have any idea of where else they might be heading?"

"No, we lost them with the bats."

"I have an idea. I might be able to pick the trail back up. Send me the footage from the pursuit right before the bats attacked. Zoom in on the car."

"Keep us informed. Owls should be picked up within thirty minutes. I'll send footage right now." The junior constable ended the call.

Constable Greene crouched down to the owls and petted the brown one's head. "Great work Constables. Great work." She said to the injured owls with a wry smile on her face.

CHAPTER
ELEVEN

Mac's chest ached. He felt a sense of despair mixed with worry and he could sense that Millie felt the same way—or perhaps he was absorbing some of her fraying nerves. He loved Millie and realized this was an affliction she suffered from time to time: intense bouts of anxiety. Anxiety that could sicken a person and cause stomach problems.

Today, he fully understood the strength of worry's toll. She certainly earned the right to worry today.

Today was not a good day.

"Millie, I understand how you feel. I really don't have a great feeling about today either." Mac kept his hands on the wheel and looked to Millie.

"Yes, usually, we're the ones hunting down the

murderers and now we're the hunted." Millie pressed two fingers above her left eye.

"Have a bad headache?"

"Trying to the stem the tide before it gets worse. Mac, what the hell happened last night? Why were you on a train from downtown Chicago in the middle of the night?"

Mac hadn't been prepared for the query. He hesitated; he felt a tremendous weight on his chest, but hoped she wouldn't be upset with him. He really didn't want to have this conversation now. He needed to bring the focus back to clearing his name. "I was just visiting my old partner, that's all. Nothing to worry about. It got late and he had a few too many, so I made sure he got home. I took the earliest train into the burbs."

Millie stayed silent. The wedding was a month away. The prep for the wedding wasn't easy and now this situation just heaped on even more stress. Mac didn't know if she would believe him. He didn't want to talk about the real reason.

He loathed silence in tense, rather tough conversations.

"Millie, there's nothing to worry about. I love you and we are getting married in a month. All will be well."

"Not if we don't clear your name. Mac, you can't fix everything. This is a serious situation. The Constabulary is not to be messed with. They probably have you and me pegged as number one suspects!"

"Are you sure we can't just go to them and say that it wasn't our fault? I'm not a magic user."

"No. The Constables in matters of dark magic are not our friends. There is no due process. Would a terrorist get due process by the Feds? No, they would not. They would be sent to some dark site and probably never found again. We'll have to figure out what happened on the train. I can check the magic world's news outlets to see if this has been reported and sent out yet. But now we don't have phones that can access the internet." Mille shook her head and shrugged her shoulders.

"We're coming up to the expressway now. We will get to 540 W Madison and see what we can find out about our victim. Someone who moves cash around all day is bound to have some enemies. If we focus on the task at hand and work like we always do together, everything will be –"

"Mac! Stop. Just drive. I need quiet right now."

Mac kept his eyes on the road and headed to downtown Chicago in his brother's minivan. He loathed the fact that it drove so smoothly. Damnit.

CHAPTER
TWELVE

The footage came through to Greene's smartphone with some visual distortion. It was enough to cause a stir of doubt, but she felt confident upon further examination that her process would work. She was the best for a reason: her methods were closely guarded trade secrets. Method's she'd honed over a course of snuffing out errant magic users and the occasional dark magic user. This particular tactic required someone with the will to enact the magic, but also the skill and power to accomplish a peculiar kind of alchemy. It was the kind of spell that narrowly avoided the distinction of being dark; very close to the type of magic she was tasked to prevent.

The magic user used bats to take down the Constabulary owls. A skill from an experienced and well-practiced user. The wand handle was stone hewn from the fjords of Norway; the stem and body of the wand was whittled from the hard wood of the Hickory tree. Stoutly constructed. Old. Passed down from previous generations of competent magic users. The witches and wizards of legend—a Viking wand.

The magic from this bat spell held traces of ancient magic. They were the traces that she had studied for years and focused her advanced degrees on.

Constable Greene smiled.

She cast her tracking spell. It was a spell she designed to trace ancient magic; it was a spell that violated the rights of magic users.

Constable Greene brought her wand to a piece of parchment she pulled from her back pocket and tapped it. A written list popped up. It was nothing spectacular; mainly, a registry of wands similar to the one she wanted to track. Only one of them was in use in the Fox River Valley. The registry list turned into a map and a singular dot appeared on her parchment. The magic user and wand were headed to Chicago.

Constable Greene was a dog with a bone.

She called the Junior Constables.

"Good job on the footage; at least I know what to look for. I also need you to check the local magic stores for the ingredients of Hear-No-Evil potions. I think that is the type of dark magic used on our train victim."

"Okay, we will let you know what we find!" The junior constables were nervous and eager to please.

Constable Greene didn't mind if they produced results. "Call me with any updates. I'm following another lead right now."

"Oh, did you pick up the trail of the suspect?"

"Not sure yet."

She lied. She knew she'd picked up the trail after the owl's failure. She didn't want anyone to know how. A registry of wands and tracking magic were yet to be approved by the Constabulary and the Coven. She didn't care.

CHAPTER
THIRTEEN

540 W. Madison: the address of one Peter Rickman's workplace and the place that Mac and Millie would start the investigation to clear Mac's name. The building was an angular construction; a triangular wedge shape, with blue tinted windows. The support beams that jutted out beyond the offices ran all the way down the sides of the building and connected to a long white column. It had a unique look and design compared to the tubular construction of the Willis Tower and the traditional skyscraper construction of the Prudential Building.

Mac and Millie entered the lobby through the rotating doors and immediately the angle of the building's design was evident. The escalators were to the right and angled up to an atrium, replete with ceiling artwork of blown glass designed to look like blue and white raindrops. There were hundreds of them and at different heights and patterns. Clearly, the main street USA vibe of Geneva contrasted greatly with the contemporary panache of a modern Chicago building.

The mystery-solving duo didn't talk for quite some time. The intensity of the early morning experiences had taken its toll. Mac readied his badge and walked to the front desk. A security guard stood behind a standing desk that spanned about twenty feet and gave way to a bank of gates used for entry into the elevator banks.

Mac held out his badge and covered the retired emblem, as usual. "Good morning, we're here just to talk to a few people in Peter Rickman's office. There has been a tragedy and we think that Mr. Rickman may have been murdered. We just need to examine his office and interview his closest work associates."

The security guard wore thick glasses. He was a tall, broad-shouldered fellow with a serious look on his face. He sighed. Hesitated.

Mac turned around and shot Millie a wide-eyed look.

The security guard cleared his throat. "Great work Officer O'Malley at the marathon. I appreciate you. Head up to the 11th floor. Should be a receptionist to greet you. You'll need these to get through the gate to the elevator bank."

"Oh, wonderful, thanks so much. I really appreciate you." Mac secured the passes with a smile.

Mac turned to Millie, who smiled.

"That was nice," Millie said.

"Yes, I thought he was going to give us a hard time. He must not know that I retired. Now let's hope we find a solid lead here." Mac responded in a hushed tone.

Millie and Mac scanned their temporary badges and walked to the elevator bank.

"Did Vince say to interview anyone specifically or no?" Millie hit the arrow up button.

There weren't too many people around. Mac looked at his watch and saw they were still a little early to be in the office. There may be a few early birds, though. Hopefully the receptionist was in already.

"He didn't. But we can just ask around. Seems like Rickman was a heavy hitter here, so he would be known. You nervous?"

"Yes, I just can't shake my nerves this time around."

"What is it? What is the feeling?" Mac asked. "Can you describe it?"

"I don't know. It feels like we're being followed."

CHAPTER
FOURTEEN

Mac and Millie walked out of the elevator and over to the reception desk. The receptionist was busy prepping badges for visitors to the floor. Evidently there was a conference today. She looked frazzled and not prepared to let in a pair of cops, fake or not.

"I will be right with you." The receptionist pulled a long string of sticky name badges from the printer.

"No problem." Mac rubbed his leg and leaned on the desk.

"Hurting a lot?" Millie whispered.

"Yes, but not too bad. Long night and now a long morning." Mac smiled, excited to do some sleuthing.

"Okay, can I help you? Oh wait, you must be the cops. The main desk downstairs just called. Go right on in; Mr. Rickman's executive assistant is just beyond the doors behind you. Sherry is her name."

"Thank you, uh, what is your name?" Mac asked.

"Candice. You can go right in."

"Thanks, Hillary." Mac said.

"Yes, thank you for your help," Millie said.

The pair of sleuths walked to the glass door with brushed metal handles. Mac opened the door and motioned for Millie to go in first. Just beyond the door and to the left was a cubicle. A young woman hammered away at her keyboard; she faced away from Mac and Millie. Sherry typed very, very fast.

Mac shook his head. "Man, I wish I could type that fast."

"Yes, you really don't type very fast at all. It took you an hour to write one page of your book. No wonder it took you so long to get it done." Millie laughed.

"At least I don't use one finger and peck at the keys like your dad does. Sheesh. Gotta gimme that at least."

"Dad and you are about the same. Pecking and all. Let's be real." Millie patted Mac's back.

"We have work to do, Mills." Mac walked to the side of Sherry's cubicle. "Sherry? Is it?"

"Oh, dear, you startled me! Sorry. Yes, I am Sherry Dachowitz. My boss just has a big meeting set for this afternoon, and I am preparing for it. He is very particular, but very effective at his job. Anyway, how can I help you two?"

Mac looked around. There weren't very many people in the office yet.

"Was just wondering if you could answer a few questions about your boss for us? Mr. Rickman, is it?"

"Yes, what is it? What happened? Who, who are you?"

"We are police officers."

Sherry's face turned white. White as snow.

Millie pointed to an empty office to the left and a better venue to break the news to her. "Would you mind if we went in the office over here? Can we use that space?" Millie asked Sherry.

"Yes, yes. That's fine. What happened?" Sherry stood up and walked to the open office. "Is Mr. Rickman okay?"

Mac and Millie followed and entered the office. The nameplate on the desk was Peter Rickman. The room was decorated with awards and charity honors. There was a philanthropic side to Mr. Rickman that he must have been very proud of and a great way to show potential clients proof of his success.

Sherry walked and sat in his chair. Mac and Millie sat across from her.

"Ms. Dachowitz, I am sorry to break this to you, but Mr. Rickman died last night." Mac just came out with it. There was no better way; he needed to rip the band-aid off.

"No. No. No. No!" Sherry screeched and slammed her head down on the desk.

Millie looked at Mac and mouthed, "Whoa."

CHAPTER
FIFTEEN

Mac took a deep breath. "I am very sorry for your loss. The best thing you can do for Peter is to help us by just answering a few questions. I take it you were close with Peter?"

Sherry breathed in and out heavily. Loudly.

"We just need to ask a few questions and we will leave you be, Sherry. I know this must be very painful. I can't imagine getting a shock like this." Millie said.

Sherry wiped away a couple tears trailing down her face. She took a deep, this time inaudible, breath.

"What can you tell us about Peter? And what was your relationship with him?" Millie continued in a calming tenor like that of a late-night talk radio host.

"He was just such a good... a good man." Sherry

exhaled and put two fingers on the bridge of her nose denoting an oncoming or current persistent headache.

"Anything else you can tell us? Any tough interactions with clients as of late?" Mac asked.

"Peter always dealt with some level of tension from certain clients. It happens in the financial investment world. No, it wasn't that. He is used to that sort of pressure and seemed to thrive on it. He loves this job and seems the happiest after he has been here a couple hours in the morning and working." Sherry said.

"What makes you say that he is happiest here? Do you spend a lot of time with him outside of work?" Millie asked.

Sherry's face turned red. "Um, no. Not like that. We rarely spend time outside of work together. I mean, we go to lunch sometimes, but that's normal. It's just that—" Sherry paused and took another deep breath.

"Just? What exactly? Any details help us understand what happened to Peter."

"He always seemed forlorn after the weekend. He never said anything about it. Never wanted to talk about things that were bothering him. He liked to keep things professional and on the level. I admired him for that, but also wished he would let people help him sometimes. We've worked together for over eight years at this point."

Mac scanned the room and did see a wall frame with multiple pictures in it. Peter and the same woman, very attractive and physically fit, in what looked like different spots around Geneva. The windmill, the courthouse, Krahams, and of course, the Tiny Wanderer.

"Do you think things were rough at home? Is that Peter's wife?" Mac pointed to the picture frame.

Sherry turned around. "Yes, that is Wendy, his wife of twenty years. I don't know how things were going for them. He never said anything, but I just got the impression he was unhappy…I did see some messages on his phone—um, I don't feel very good. I need to go to the bathroom. Excuse me." Sherry ran out of the office.

Mac and Millie looked at each other.

"She saw messages on his phone. Like she was going through his phone?" Millie furrowed her brow.

"Yeah, I mean she stopped herself and then just ran out of here. Why don't you see how she's doing in the bathroom? I will check out her desk and see if I can find anything strange. She seems overly attached to her boss—who kept things strictly professional." Mac gripped his cane and pushed himself up from the chair.

"I'll check on her. Be right back. I have no idea where the restroom is; I'll ask the receptionist." Millie walked out.

Mac walked to the cubicle just outside of Peter Rickman's full office. Sherry had no pictures on her desk. Very neat. Very clean. Incredibly organized. Meticulous down to the way her screens were set up. Every screen was perfectly queued up to start a busy day at work: her calendar, to-do list, and email. There were a few drawers. Mac opened the top drawer.

Inside the perfectly organized drawer was a small envelope. Stationery akin to a thank you card size lay open and just spilled over the crease to seal the envelope. Mac grabbed it.

"Hey! Can I help you? Have you seen Peter this morning?" A deep bellowing voice rang out from behind him.

Mac shoved the thank you note into his jacket pocket and turned around.

"Hello, I'm sorry. I haven't seen Peter." Mac looked at a tall, but thin, man, whose deep voice didn't match the physique.

"Where's Sherry? I need to see Rickman now. He

jumped on one of my deals last minute that son of a bitch." The tall thin man's chest heaved.

Mac pulled out his badge. "Do you want to step into his office? I need to ask you a few questions."

"A fucking cop. Hell no. You can talk to my lawyer before I answer any of your questions." Thin man turned around to walk out of the office and back to the elevator.

Mac didn't hesitate. "Peter Rickman is dead and we suspect foul play. Either talk to me now or you will be visited by more people just like me who'll bring you down to the Geneva police station."

The thin man stopped. He let out a huge sigh and turned back to Mac.

Millie walked into the room. "Mac, she's gone. I can't find Sherry anywhere."

CHAPTER
SIXTEEN

"Well, that gives one pause. Doesn't it? Um, could you—or would you—mind taking a seat inside Peter's office, Mister...?" Mac pointed with his cane to the office indicating the thin man join him.

"McGuire. Pat McGuire. I have a 10am appointment so you'd better make this quick." Pat walked into the office and sat down.

Mac took the gorilla position behind the desk. "Pat, you seem awfully upset with Mr. Rickman this morning. Tell me about your relationship with Peter." Mac ran his hand over the smooth top of the desk.

"I was on his team for years under his tutelage. I didn't learn much because he didn't tell me much. He was a 'lead by example' type, but for someone trying to make it in this gig, that's a bit tough. Obviously, I didn't kill him if I was storming in to see him this morning. I had no idea." Pat had slicked back hair and he looked the part of the slimy salesman versus a cold-blooded killer...but Mac didn't assume anything.

"What exactly is done here? What is this job?" Mac asked. "Pretty fancy office up here."

"We are a PE firm. The most successful in Chicago." Pat shook his head as if Mac should have known already.

"I am sorry, I'm just a homicide detective. What exactly is a PE firm?"

"A private equity investment firm. We handle high-profile clients' assets and manage their portfolio. Listen, I don't have time to go over this with you." Pat lifted off the seat.

Mac brought his cane out to the top of the desk. "Um, wait, Pat. We still don't want an embarrassing visit by a few uniformed policemen later today, right? Certainly, won't want to disrupt your 10am with a high-profile client. Sit. Stay a bit longer."

Millie stood in the doorway to block Peter.

"Ridiculous." Pat sat back down and gripped the armrest until his knuckles turned white.

"Patty, when you walked in here you were very upset with Peter. Can you elaborate?" Mac smiled.

"Yes, he poached one of my clients: a client I brought in when I still worked on his team. The client was supposed to stay with me and be one of my first whales when I would have the chance to start my own team and build out my book. Of course, I'm upset. Peter was a dick. But I wouldn't kill him. I just wanted an explanation and a chance to take MY client back."

"You don't think any of Peter's clients would be upset with him, do you?"

"No, Peter showed them his best side and all his energy went to his clients. I seriously doubt that."

"Would you say you have a lot of pent-up rage and frustration towards your former boss, Pat? I mean, that is what I am feeling from you right now. Officer Paderson, are you picking up on those vibes too?" Mac looked at Millie in the doorway.

"Vibes aren't great, Officer O'Malley. Not great." Millie shook her head.

"Jesus Christ. Why would I come into his office to talk to him the morning after he was murdered? If I killed him, wouldn't I want to be as far away as possible?"

"I don't know, you tell me." Mac sat back in the chair.

Pat McGuire put up his hands. Mac had rendered him speechless.

Mac watched him squirm. "Let's just get back to basics. Where were you this morning at about 5am?"

"I was at my apartment in the West Loop 727 West Madison. Sleeping. Check with the security staff at the front desk. Can I go now?" Pat asked.

"A disgruntled co-worker. Big money clients at risk. A guy with the means to pay people to do dirty work for him. Things aren't looking too good for you, Pat. We will see you soon." Mac waved him towards the door.

"Fuck off." Pat rushed out the door nearly knocking into Millie, who stepped to the side.

Millie walked in and sat down. "This has been an interesting office visit."

"Sherry and Pat both have very strong feelings about our victim. Very strong feelings, which reminds me." Mac pulled out the note card from his jacket pocket.

"What do we do about Sherry's abrupt exit?"

"We will have Vince look up where she lives and we will follow up with her later. I found this in her desk drawer. It says, *Dear Peter, I had a lovely time at dinner last night. Thanks again for the wonderful meal and even better company. I can't help but feel there is something more between us than just a professional rela-*

tionship. Do you feel the same? XO XO Sherry." Mac frowned and rubbed his forehead.

"Could we have two disgruntled co-workers? Both with motives?" Millie asked.

"The ink on this card doesn't look fresh. She could have kept this in her desk for a long time. Both are solid leads. We also need to get back to Geneva and meet with the wife. I am sure GPD already has, but maybe we can act as CPD to her, or we can have Vince question the wife. Either way, we have work to do." Mac stood up from the desk and planted his cane in the thin office carpet.

Millie turned around and faced the window. Her purse shook on her hip. She didn't think she turned the burner phone on vibrate. She opened her purse; something else vibrated.

Her wand.

"Mac, we have a problem."

Three more workers walked into the office from the reception area. The workday was gearing up to start. Millie's wand vibrated for some strange reason; she turned back around and walked toward Mac. He was about to leave Peter's office and, as she approached him, the wand stopped vibrating. She turned back to the window—it started to undulate again.

"What's happening? What is that buzzing sound?" Mac asked.

Millie walked to the window and looked out at the surrounding buildings: the Presidential Towers were to the left with a four-story parking garage attached to it. Millie scanned the buildings and then looked to the top floor of the parking garage. A figure stood on the roof of the empty garage; a woman in a black leather jacket looked outward and it felt like she stared directly at Millie.

"Mac, we have to go now. We gotta get far away from here—now." Millie turned around.

"What? What is going on?"

"It's the Constabulary. Somehow, they found us."

CHAPTER
SEVENTEEN

"How on earth? Didn't we lose the owls?" Mac looked over Millie's shoulder and out the window.

"We did. My wand is vibrating. That is Constable Greene. I know her and we were in the same magic academy class. She was a hardass—a serious woman back then. Maybe she somehow traced my wand? Every wand has privacy protective spells on them like our phones do. I don't get it." Millie gripped her purse, but didn't take the wand out for fear of spooking the workers still entering the office.

"We gotta get rid of the wand and fast." Mac shook his head and hobbled out of the office and back toward the elevator bank.

"I have an idea. We need to hang on to it for a bit

longer." Millie followed Mac. She pushed the elevator button. "Let's get downstairs."

"We'll check the parking lot first and if the Constable has that covered, we head left and exit out the Washington Boulevard side, away from Presidential Towers. Then we head toward the river." Mac let the middle elevator's passengers exit before entering the car.

"Sounds good. Mac, your leg. If we need to run, can you handle it?"

"I—it might be tough, but in short bursts I can. Yes."

"I am going to temporarily relieve your leg pain. It can last up to five or six hours or so.."

"Similar to painkillers? If it's without the addiction, then do it! Why haven't we done this the whole time we've known each other?" Mac looked surprised.

"It's not a cure for your leg and it saps your energy way too much as it wears off. Magic is effective, but it's unpredictable. In this instance, though, I say we give it a shot." Millie pointed her wand at Mac's leg.

"We can do it. But, you know, before we do—"

"Temporarus Curo!" Millie said aloud just as the elevator door opened to the first floor.

A young woman held her Starbricks latte and

looked very confused just outside the elevator door's threshold.

"Holy cow. That feels great! I mean, that looks great. Your drink, I mean." Mac rubbed his leg and looked toward the confused woman. The pair of sleuths exited the elevator.

"Excuse me. Sorry. He just really loves Starbricks. Have a great day!" Millie addressed the confused woman while stuffing her wand back into her purse.

Mac and Millie turned left. Mac had more pep in his step—a sudden jolt of energy mixed with a pain-free leg pushed him forward in a gleeful, excited manner. He turned toward the exit—

But he halted and turned back toward the elevator bank.

"It's Jackson. My brother's partner. Shit." Mac exhaled and his high from Millie's pain eradication spell dissipated as quickly as it came. Detective Jackson stood in front of the reception desk. He flashed his badge. The security guard was different this time; not the same as who let Mac and Millie in.

Millie kept pace with Mac and followed him.

"What do we do?" Millie asked. She rubbed her head as if she felt a migraine coming on.

There was a hallway behind the elevator banks

that led to the building's gym to the right and probably conference rooms or a cafeteria to the left.

"Let's head right and just walk. If we wait a bit, he will have to go up the elevator and we can slip out."

"Can't we just talk to Jackson? Isn't he your brother's partner?"

"Yeah, in a perfect world, we could and should be able to talk to him. But my brother and Officer Jackson don't get along: Jackson is ambitious and is concerned about looking good and moving forward with his career. My brother just wants to do his police work. They have different approaches and he probably views cracking this case without Vince as a boost to his career advancement." Mac walked to the end of the hall and stepped onto an escalator. It only led up one floor towards the café.

"Where are we going?" Millie gripped the rubber banister of the escalator.

"We're going up and down real quick. Like I used to do at Marshall Fields at Christmastime when I was a kid. He should be cleared and up the elevator by the time we get back down."

"This is dumb." Millie laughed.

"Probably, yes." Mac smiled, pain-free.

CHAPTER
EIGHTEEN

Mac and Millie rode the escalator back to the first floor and made their way past the elevator bank; both looked for Detective Jackson. Nowhere to be found. The guard must have let him go upstairs.

"Coast is clear," Millie said.

"Hang a left and head towards the Washington Street exit. I must admit, I do feel great. Thanks Millie. Kinda makes me want to just get addicted to painkillers and call it."

"Yeah, we should just get you addicted to drugs right before the wedding. That would be perfect."

"Sweet. I busted my fair share of dealers, so we should stop and see them. I'm sure some of them have served their sentence already." Mac cracked a wry smile.

They rode down the escalators to the ground floor and made their way out of 540 W Madison.

The blustery wind smacked their faces hard. The cold sent shivers down Mac's spine, but he noted that the cold didn't cause the usual pain spike in his leg. It felt great. Restored.

"Mac, you really should try to use the cane still. The pain is still there. You're just numb to it, which means your leg is still suffering from the same physical damage it always does. So just be careful not to cause more damage, is what I'm saying." Millie looked at him. She was clearly concerned.

"Way to be a buzzkill." Mac twirled and danced in the street with his cane like Gene Kelly in a musical. He even spun around the nearest light post.

"Mac, just use the damn cane!" Millie growled.

Mac took a deep breath. A rush of anger filled him. "Leave me be, Millie. Let me enjoy this—if only for a very short amount of time." He stopped his spin.

"I'm sorry." Millie followed Mac as he rushed ahead toward the lot where they'd parked the minivan.

Mac turned around and nearly bumped into Millie.

"Mac! What are you doing?!" Millie reeled from Mac grabbing her arm.

"She's in the lot. She hasn't seen me yet. The lady on the building." Mac whispered. "Your wand. We need to get rid of it."

Millie turned around with him. A car approached with a rideshare sticker on it; a man waiting with his phone out was checking the license plate. She pulled the wand from her purse as they walked and waited for the opportune moment. The middle-aged, bearded man opened the back passenger door of the Cadillac Escalade and Millie acted like she slipped and placed the wand underneath the front passenger seat.

"Hey, this is my ride, lady!" The bearded man yelled.

"Relax, she just fell. It's all yours, pal. You okay, honey?" Mac helped Millie up.

"So sorry. Yes, it's yours. I just slipped." Millie wiped loose strands of white hair from her face.

"Christ." The bearded man's voice faded as Mac and Millie made their way east down Washington toward the Chicago River.

"That should keep her busy for a while." Millie smiled.

"Great work." Mac rubbed Millie's hand.

"Millie Paderson! Hey Millie! Is that you?" The familiar voice of Constable Greene rang out and racked their ears.

Mac and Millie didn't turn around. They just ran as fast as they could; hurtling towards the Chicago River.

CHAPTER NINETEEN

Millie Paderson. Constable Greene couldn't believe it. The goody-two shoes, Suzy Magic Academy, Prom Queen ran from the Constabulary. Millie Paderson, in many ways, was not only Constable Greene's arch-rival, but also her object of envy. She had to admit she liked Millie. Millie was never mean to anyone. She was beloved by all and, eventually, did win over the one-day Constable Greene. The Constable just didn't like the popularity contests at Upper Magic Academy in general, and dumb traditions like elections of a prom court drove her mad.

Millie and her companion with a cane ran with considerable speed. Was the cane just being used as an accessory, like in antebellum America? He certainly moved like he didn't have any use for it. The cane could have very well bludgeoned the victim on the train, although Greene thought the wounds could have been caused by other, darker means. She just needed to talk to them. Why the running? Perhaps Greene's own reputation preceded her, and Millie figured out the use of forbidden magic would incur harsh punishment. She wasn't wrong.

Constable Greene kept pace with the pair of suspects as they ran up a hill; it led to the Washington Bridge over the Chicago River. The Constable, confident in her training and tip top shape, would have them within the next thirty seconds. She hadn't even tapped into second gear yet.

MILLIE STRUGGLED to keep pace with Mac. Not that Mac ran faster than her—it was the opposite. Millie's long legs, quick twitch muscles, and general athletic ability naturally emasculated Mac. She couldn't help that even with a pain-free leg, he moved like a turtle. The hare that was Constable Greene gained on them.

Millie felt the metal of the bridge rattle under their feet. "Mac, you have to move faster."

"I'm giving it all I got." Mac heaved and yelled.

"If Candice gets us, we're done. She's the toughest

Constable there is. I was worried we might have attracted the attention of Constabulary's top cop. Shit!" Millie nearly ran into another female jogger with earphones on.

"The Civic Opera House is on the right. When we get there, hide behind the columns! She won't see us!" Mac held his cane in his right hand and felt pressure from both his front and rear. He was struggling to keep pace with Millie while being pursued by the aggressive Constable.

Millie was glad to see a large group of ten or twelve people heading over the bridge toward whatever building they were headed to on the west side of the river. It would help obscure Candice's vision for now as they made the right turn.

Mac had told the truth: a long block of Greco-Roman columns led all the way down to Madison. They could take a breather behind one and maybe lose her.

Millie made the turn first. Mac followed.

"Let's get to the middle!" Mac pointed his cane at Millie, a good ten paces ahead of him.

Millie already put her back against the tan pillar and looked to Mac. So far, no sign of Constable Greene, but she couldn't be too far off. She'd hoped the group of commuters slowed her down enough for Mac to make it.

"Come on Mac!" Millie peeked out from behind the column and looked at Mac. It felt like he moved in slow motion. Slowest person ever.

Constable Greene entered Millie's vision at the corner of Washington and Wacker. She seemed frustrated and stopped. She looked for a sign of Mac and Millie, as she knew they weren't ahead of her anymore. They must have taken a turn.

Millie cringed and pulled back; feeling the safety of the column.

"Mills." Mac said.

"Ah!" Millie screamed and then covered her mouth.

Mac stood next to her behind the column.

"She's at the corner. She stopped—she knows we must have turned." Millie whispered.

A few people passed by them and observed the couple huddled with their backs against the column. Mac's chest heaved. Millie didn't breathe as deeply.

"Okay, do I peek?" Mac whispered.

"No, you idiot. Let me do it. Your head is giant."

"Fair enough. But your neck is super long like the brachiosaur from Jurassic Park. Just sayin'."

Millie looked out from the opposite side of the

column. Greene looked pissed; hands on her hips. She looked north and then south toward Mac and Millie.

Then she started walking in their direction.

Millie pulled her head behind the column. "Here she comes."

CHAPTER
TWENTY

Mac looked at the sidewalk and the columns that led down to Madison Street. Traffic on Wacker was slow, only a few cars here and there, but stopping a vehicle in its tracks would most likely cause the driver to beep and give away their location. The area was empty somehow—of all the times to happen, a bustling morning commute died right at the same moment a relentless Constable pursued them. There were no people to help cover their tracks; obscure the Constable's vision.

And none to give them a way out of the situation.

The Constable's footsteps could be heard. She walked slowly, but with a purpose: probably examining the back of each column she'd passed. The sound bounced between the columns and the Civic Opera House.

"Mills, we have to time this just right." Mac whispered.

The footfalls sounded closer, but not close enough to prompt a move by the mystery-solving duo. Then suddenly she stopped. There were no more footsteps.

"What is she doing?" Mac asked.

"I don't know; let me look." Millie peeked back towards Washington Street.

"Well..."

"She's examining a small piece of paper?. I know what she's doing! If she really did track my wand, then the paper shows the wand's location. Maybe she thinks we're still with the wand. She lost sight of us.It's the smart move." Millie said.

"That is so cool. How do we get one of those?" Mac whispered.

The footsteps resumed and grew louder as the Constable got closer. Mac and Millie huddled together. They both knew they would have to move around the column as the Constable passed. They held each other's hands and listened. Waited.

Stomp! Stomp! Constable Greene walked with a commanding, intimidating purpose. Her gait signaled her rage and frustration.

She drew nearer.

She was very, very close.

Mac and Millie slowly rotated out towards Wacker Drive.

Then the stomps ceased. They heard a scrape across the ground; the audible rap of the Constable's pounding boots gradually softened. She walked in the opposite direction, back towards Washington.

"She's going away." Millie let out an audible sigh.

"Yes, it sounds like it." Mac looked at the sidewalk and a few people populated the path once more. Probably just the usual streetlight stop-and-go. He took a deep breath.

"That was too close. I don't' know if I could handle this. How did you handle being in intense situations as a cop?" Millie asked.

"You get used to it after a while, but usually I'm the one pursuing a suspect like the Constable pursued us. Not the other way around."

Millie peeked out from behind the column once more. She could see the Constable walking further into the Loop, crossing Wacker Drive on Washington Street. "Okay, we are good to move. What now?"

"Let's just get back to the minivan in the 540-parking lot and get back to Geneva. We need to talk to Mrs. Rickman—and fast."

"Your brother said we shouldn't go back to Geneva right now. That would be pretty dumb, wouldn't it?" Millie joined Mac walking toward Madison Street.

"Ah damnit. Yes, yes, it would be. We need to check out 727 W Madison first. To see if Pat, our disgruntled co-worker's alibi, checks out. But even if it's only a couple blocks away, we need to take the minivan so we can roll quickly if needed. Leave the car running out in front. Shouldn't take me too long."

"We can call Vince to see what he can find out about Mrs. Rickman. Plus, I have an idea: we can check if any of these people close to Peter are magic users. We can have my parents check the registry."

"Registry of magic users?"

Mille nodded. "Yes, someone used dark magic last night in Geneva and Peter wound up dead. There could be a connection and now we have a few names we can run through the registry."

"Yes, and where the hell did Sherry run off to? There's still that strange behavior to examine. We are in the thick of it now. Let's hope Jackson isn't done upstairs. We still have to watch for him. I'll call Vince now." Mac flipped the black plastic burner phone open. The old school beeping audio comforted Mac and forced thoughts of simpler times.

CHAPTER
TWENTY-ONE

Vince O'Malley paced the sidewalk just east of the Geneva Police Station. He felt useless. His brother's dilemma had become his dilemma. He'd never been removed from a case before in his twenty-three-year career—until Mac became the prime suspect in a gruesome murder on the Union Pacific railroad's Geneva Express train. He didn't want to go home yet. He just paced up and down, trying to think of an excuse for heading back into the station.

His phone buzzed. A number he didn't recognize… but could possibly be Mac.

"Hello, this is Detective O'Malley."

"Vincey, this is Officer O'Malley."

"Retired, Mac. Retired. And in deep shit." Vince shook his head and stopped pacing.

"We need you to check out Rickman's wife. We found some interesting things out here at his office. The marriage, perhaps, wasn't in the best shape. If you could roll to her house; that would be great."

"Yeah, I'll try. Jackson was already there this morning—which reminds me. You might want to look out. I'm sure he is headed down there if he isn't already there."

"We saw him. He was in the office lobby when we were heading downstairs. He didn't see us. Let me know what you find out from the wife. I don't even know her name," Mac said.

"Wendy. Peter and Wendy. J.M Barrie is pleased, I'm sure. Jeez, this day just gets stranger and stranger. I'll let you know what I find out. I have their address; I can head there now."

"How long do you think we should steer clear of the area?"

"Mac, until we can prove your innocence, that's when. Stay far away from here. You should just take the minivan to Tennessee or something. Jackson won't stop until he finds you and brings you in for questioning. The problem is he wants it wrapped up quick. He's got a train car full of passengers pegging you at the scene."

"Yes, a bunch of drunken idiots."

"Yes, I understand that. The blood everywhere spewing from the side of his head and you holding a cane over him doesn't look good either. I will see what I can find out about the wife. Did you find out anything else useful, or no?" Vince asked hand on hip. He didn't realize how tired he was. The caffeine had worn off.

"Yes, some possible leads: a disgruntled employee of his and a lovesick assistant. Will keep you in the loop? Thanks again, Vincey. I owe you one." Mac ended the call.

Vince forced his hand into his pocket and pulled out his notepad. He flipped for the Rickman's address, surprisingly not far from the famed Third Street. It was probably a big, beautiful home not unlike the home of the deceased owner of the Tiny Wanderer.

Millie kept the minivan running as Mac entered 727 W Madison Street. A beautiful new blue tinted glass high-rise cylinder, shaped like someone stepped on the cardboard center of your favorite Christmas wrapping paper, hung from the ceiling.

Mac opened the door to a mosaic of tiles cascading in different shades of sapphire to indigo, all detailing the street address; *727*. There was no denying that he'd entered the right building. The receptionist sat only a few paces away from the mosaic. Greeted him. Clearly not remembering his face before.

"Good morning. May I help you, sir?" The receptionist stood from behind her small one-person desk in front of the elevator bank. Natural light poured in from every direction. The sitting area on the left of the desk only had eight chairs. They apparently did not encourage large group gatherings in the lobby. A smart move. A secure move.

Mac realized she probably didn't have an RFID scan when he entered. Nowadays residents can choose to wear a band, a keychain, or the traditional card to grant them access to elevator banks. The RFID system gave the security team and the receptionist a detailed report of the person entering including a picture.

"Yes, Hello! How are you this morning?" Mac smiled.

She returned his smile with a toothy grin of her own. "I am well. How about yourself?"

"Great. Feeling refreshed. My coffee has kicked in and I am ready to start the day. Anyway, I was wondering if you could help me with an investigation. I am currently the active detective on a homicide." Mac brought out the trusty retired badge.

"Oh dear. Yes, what is it." She sat back down ready to help, probably eager to do something besides playing mobile puzzlers on her phone on—on the phone that fell to the ground when she stood.

"Hi, I am Officer O'Malley. Pat McGuire: was he home yesterday at all? Did he sleep here last night? Is there a way you can check that?"

"Yes, I saw Mr. McGuire leave the building this morning. I can also check his entry and exit profile on our system. Oh dear, a homicide?" The receptionist sat down and pounded her keyboard.

"Thanks for your prompt help. I do appreciate it." Mac ignored her further questioning of the homicide.

"Mr. McGuire entered the building at 9:08pm and exited the building this morning. Hope this helps."

"Did anyone leave the building during the night?"

The receptionist hammered the keyboard once again.

"No. It was a very quiet night. The building hasn't sold to capacity yet either. We are only at about 30% occupancy as of now."

"Okay, again, I appreciate the help." Mac turned around and headed back out the door—

He saw Jackson's unmarked squad car heading towards the building. Luckily Mac's leg still felt the effects of Millie's spell. He sprinted out of the lobby and back to the minivan. He pulled the sliding door open and flung himself into the car. "Millie! Get your head down. Jackson's squad is going to pass us in a second!"

"Oh gosh!" Millie leaned toward the center console and armrest.

"Just keep down. Hopefully he doesn't recognize Vince's stupid minivan!" Mac yelled.

"Why are you being so loud? Shush or I will kill you. My headache has been lingering. He probably passed us already, you idiot."

"Sorry. The windows are tinted back here. I'll check." Mac pulled himself up from between the two middle seats and looked out.

"Well, my neck hurts. Can we please get out of here?" Millie said from her awkward leaning position. Her right shoulder lay on the center armrest.

"Yes, yes, let's roll. And it's not my fault you have a brachiosaurus neck!"

"Where we headed?"

"Let's head south until we hear from Vince. No reason for any of the authorities to head south." Mac climbed his way into the front seat. His leg was fully functional.

CHAPTER
TWENTY-TWO

Vince hoofed it over to the Rickman household on 4th and Fulton. It was a large colonial with yellow-siding and a wrap-around porch. An orange Ford Bronco was in the driveway. Vince walked up the steps; they creaked louder than he'd anticipated. He rapped on the door with his knuckles.

No answer.

He knocked once more.

Still nothing.

He examined the doorframe for signs of a doorbell when the door opened.

A brunette woman faced him from behind the storm door.

"Hello, Geneva Police Department. I know we've

already been here this morning, but I had a few more questions for you." Vince smiled.

"Oh, I'm certain you don't have any more questions for me. I'm Wendy's sister. I really don't think she is up for more questions right now. Can this wait until tomorrow? It is just a lot for her to process, as you can imagine." The sister said. She still held the storm door closed.

"I am sure the shock must be overwhelming. I understand. It's just that we are getting close to a cause of death but need to shore up a few more details. That's all."

"Listen Officer. She is absolutely devastated. She is sleeping right now. I am not waking her; you'll just have to come back later." The sister began to close the door.

"Hey, wait, don't you work at Mulberry's Dry cleaners? I pick up my shirts from you. I thought I recognized you!" Vince smiled more, knowing it irritated this woman.

"Yes, Geneva really isn't that big of a town. I do work there and yes; I know who you are too. Find your brother and this will all be cleared up. The other officers, that nice Detective Jackson, warned us you might come by. You bring your brother in—he killed my brother-in-law. How dare you?"

"Well—"

The sister cut him off. She shut the door in Vince's face.

"Thanks so much, fricking Debbie." Vince turned back and descended the creaky steps. Debbie Positano: resident dry cleaner and prominent Geneva gossiper. Always dishing. Always telling stories about her clients.

No way he could get to Wendy Rickman with her in the way. Shit.

CHAPTER
TWENTY-THREE

Hank paced when he was anxious. Many people do, but his pacing brought things to a different level. A constant loop around the front room to the dining room; back and forth all while looking out the windows. He had both his hips replaced from years of climbing up and down ladders and scaffolding, installing the siding on people's homes all over the Fox River Valley. He enjoyed his work. Being a carpenter provided for his family and gave Millie and her siblings a great start to their lives. The physical toll, in Hank's mind, was worth it.

"Hey Beck. Any word from her?"

"No John, and you asked about thirty seconds

ago." Beck's voice could be heard from the couch in the living room.

"Should I try and call her again, or no?" Hank walked like someone who had had their hips replaced. There was a stiffer movement to his gait, not the full motion many take advantage of and don't even think about.

"I don't know why you ask if you're going to do whatever you want, Hanni." It was Becca's nickname for Hank: Hanni, like Yanni the New Age composer but, with an H.

"I will try her one more time. Why would the cops come to our house asking about her and Mac?! I still don't get it."

The basement door creaked open. Grandma Jo, Becca's Mom, emerged from the stairwell.

"The news is saying that Mac is the prime suspect for a murder on the Geneva Express late last night." Grandma Jo, like Mac, used a cane.

"Mother, are you serious? Are you sure you didn't dream it? I saw you asleep on the chair, like, ten minutes ago." Becca raised herself from the couch in the living room.

"It's all over the news Becky!" Grandma Jo said.

"Well, there's your explanation Hanni." Becca said.

Hank's rapid pace brought him into the living room with his wife and mother-in-law.

"We knew they must have been in some kind of trouble since the cops paid us a visit this morning, but they didn't mention any of that!" Hank yelled; he was hyped.

"Hank, if you keep yelling, I will kill you. Mom, did the news report say anything else?" Beck reached for her phone on the desk. It started to ring.

"It could be Millie!" Hank yelled.

Beck threw a pillow from the couch at Hank's head. She nailed him square in the face.

"Hello, who is this?" Beck answered, her speech fast.

The phone was on speaker.

"Mom, it's me Millie. Sorry if you didn't recognize the number. We had to get rid of our phones. Mac is in trouble—and so am I. We are being hunted down by both the cops and the Constabulary. Mac was just in the wrong place at the wrong time. Sorry, we just don't have a lot of time to talk. Could you do us a favor and check the magic-user registry for us? Vince is talking to Mac right now. Mac, what are the names again?" Millie's voice trailed off. The audible hum of a car engine made the entire conversation just that much more faint than usual.

"Okay, let me grab a pen and paper. Real quick." Becca walked into the kitchen and opened a side drawer: it was filled with pens, crayons, and scrap paper for the grandkids. She heard Mac's mumbled voice in the background.

Hank followed Becca into the kitchen and put both hands on the granite counter of the island in the middle of the large room.

"Wendy and Peter Rickman. Debbie Positano. Sherry Dachowitz and Pat McGuire. Just check those names and let us know if they are magic users or not. We have reason to believe dark magic was used to kill the person on the train. Did you guys get that Dark Magic alert this morning too?"

"Yes, we did." Hank said loudly, trying to get his voice to register in Beck's phone.

"Hank! Stop yelling. We all can hear you. We will get back to you soon. Okay, Millie, please be careful. Are you guys going to head back in this direction? Where are you?"

"We are still on the road. Vince said it wasn't safe to come back into the area. Until we figure out who killed Peter Rickman on the train, we have to keep moving. Love you guys. Talk to you later."

"Love you too. Be safe." Becca ended the call.

Millie's words weighed heavily on them. The

possibility that their daughter may not be able to safely return home was devastating. A heavy cloud hung over the room.

"Where the hell did we put the registry, Beck?" Hank threw his hands up.

"Probably in the butler's pantry in one of the drawers. We will find it." Becca walked into a small area between the kitchen and the dining room. The butler's pantry traditionally was a staging area for lavish dinners; the various entrees would be waiting in this small area to be served to the guests at the table. In the Paderson household, it held bills, various piles of junk mail, and just about anything else you could think of. It ebbed and flowed with how much crap would be on it at any given time, however, at Christmas time it always held delicious desserts, candies, cookies, and culinary delights that Becca gorged herself with.

"Gosh, I can't believe all the crap on here, Beck. We have got to clean this up." Hank rifled through the drawers.

Then it happened.

Dust billowed from the drawers and Hank started sneezing.

"Achoo!" Hank covered his mouth and then

excused himself from the butler's pantry. He walked into the kitchen and let out another sneeze.

"Oh, here we go. Hanni, get a hold of yourself!"

"Achoo!"

"Three—there will be about ten more, Mom. It drives me nuts!" Becca picked up a few bills and then put them back down.

"Achoo! Achoo! Acho!"

"Becky, he can't help it." Grandma Jo leaned on her cane and walked to the pantry to look as well.

"Do you have one downstairs, Mom?' Becca piled the contents of a drawer onto the counter.

"Here it is." Grandma Jo opened the cabinet door above the counter.

She grabbed a nondescript leather-bound book out. It had no etching and no names; it looked like just an old journal.

"Achoo! Great you found it! Achoo! Sorry!"

CHAPTER
TWENTY-FOUR

Constable Greene pulled the wand out from the large black SUV on the corner of Grand and Michigan. She grimaced and looked north to the twin spires of the John Hancock building. She needed to get out of Downtown Chicago—and fast. Her wand-tracing spell needed work. Millie's wand must have tipped her off. Even now, she could feel the wand vibrate in her hand. A risky, bold move to use that type of magic, but still: she wanted and needed to find Millie and her companion.

"Excuse me, ma'am. Need a ride? You'll have to book from the app." The SUV driver walked out of a Starbricks with a cup of coffee.

"No, no thanks." Constable Greene walked away and headed South toward the river.

She thought about going home for a nap. Maybe even a quick shower; she could even see her building from where she was. Still, she had more work to do. She hadn't gotten anywhere with the case yet and had expended a lot of energy.

Her phone buzzed in her interior jacket pocket.

"Make any progress?" Constable Greene's voice was more aggressive than usual: harried and frustrated. Maybe she really should nap.

"We have checked and cleared Millie Paderson and her family of any wrongdoing. All of them cleared. There's nothing at all that would make us think they would even begin to use dark magic." The young constable's voice cracked in her. He talked fast.

"Please tell me you have more. What about the Hear-No-Evil theory?"

"Some interesting purchases were flagged on the underground market that were traced to someone in the Chicago area. We only know there was activity there. Someone blocked the Constabulary from finding the contents of the purchases with a roving spell. It kept giving us nonsense and made our tracking magic very confused and, frankly, useless."

"So, there was flagged activity. That is interesting." Constable Greene felt a tinge of hope. The underground magic market always had activity, but it was mostly harmless substances, ingredients, and spell books banned in the USA: nothing that would cause the tracking magic spell to flag a purchase. Flagged purchases usually meant a combination of liveries that could potentially cause harm.

"Sorry, I don't have much more than that." The rookie's voice trembled.

"Good work, Constable." Greene ended the call. She knew exactly where to go next.

Monk's Pub. Dieter would have some information for her.

205 W Lake wasn't that far of a walk. She wished she could use broom flight, but not in the middle of the city in the daylight. She looked back at the black SUV and thought about paying for the ride. Why not.

Mac and Millie made it to the Southside in quick fashion on a reverse commute down the Dan Ryan expressway.

"This is my old stomping grounds. I grew up down here, Millie. Had a great childhood. So many kids, families, and a common bond of Catholic school right down the street." Mac pointed to a small Chicago bungalow with orange brick and a green awning. It was small, probably only 900 square feet.

"Oh, this is so cool, Mac. Why haven't you shown me this yet?" Millie looked out the window.

"Geneva is such a great place. And this is a pretty far drive. I thought about giving you a tour one day. It's a little different from the palatial 272 WitchHazel! Haha!" Mac joked.

"True, but this is great. Thanks for taking me here. It's distracting me from our situation."

"Yes, the house was small, but there are so many fond memories here. We would host Christmas and have, like, fifty people jammed into the basement. It was chaotic, awesome, and just plain fun. My cousins would sneak upstairs and start unwrapping my family's gifts to each other—which, of course, were not meant for them. They had a ton of gifts downstairs just for them, but they were little and didn't know any better."

"That is hilarious."

"Then, they would write on the walls with markers and break all my toys and destroy my room. It was madness, but I loved it. Then eventually the whole O'Malley clan would leave, and it was just the five of us left to open the gifts to each other. We gathered around the Christmas tree in our tiny living room; it was taken up mostly by the giant tree Mom always bought." Mac's eyes glossed over. Tears welled in his eyes.

He stared at his old house with a pondering, nostalgic look.

"Sounds like you truly had wonderful memories here, Mac." Millie grabbed his hand.

"I really wish you could have met Mom. She would have loved you very much. Which I don't get because you're just okayish." Mac smiled.

"Right! I am mediocre at best." Millie laughed.

"No, seriously, she would have loved you like her daughter and she really was a wonderful human being. I was very fortunate to have her as a mother."

"Speaking of parents." Millie grabbed the flip phone that rang from the side door compartment.

"Hello Millie!" It was her dad's voice loud enough for both Mac and Millie to hear.

"Hello Dad, anything pop up in the registry?"

"We checked the Rickmans. We checked the Dachowitz lady and the McGuire—"

"Get to the point Hank!" Beck's voice burst through the receiver.

"Oh boy." Mac's eyes went wide.

"Positano family is listed as magic users in the area. Also, the Dachowitz family showed up as well, but they haven't had an active registry in many years.

Debbie Positano is a current magic user. Does that help?" Becca said.

"Yes, Mom, it does help. Thank you. It gives us another lead to follow for sure."

"Honey, please be careful. We are worried sick over here. Is there anything else we can do?"

"No, that's good for now, Mom. Love you, Mom."

"Love you too. Be safe!"

Millie ended the call. She reached over and hugged Mac. "Mac, are you sure everything is okay with us? You were just visiting your old partner, but it just seems like an odd thing to do that so late; in the middle of the night. Are you sure you aren't having second thoughts?"

Mac squeezed her tight in front of his childhood home. "Millie, I love you and want to spend the rest of my life with you. Was part of me revisiting my old life to say goodbye to it? Yes. Probably. I am a nostalgic guy. I know that my future isn't here; it isn't being a hero cop in the big city anymore. I lived that dream and now I get to live out the dream of having you as my wife in the quaint town of Geneva. Starting fresh, doing my book tours, and spending time with you and our families. You are my everything. My new partner and a partner for life."

"Okay. I want that too. I really wish you wouldn't

have been on that train last night, you giant idiot." Millie snickered.

"Hahaha! Me too. Enough of this mushy stuff. We have a murder to solve, Mills."

"And we have to clear our names, too. There's that."

"Yes, of course. We gotta get back to Geneva. Time to visit the Positanos—no matter what." Mac started the car. He took one more look at his childhood home.

And he smiled.

CHAPTER
TWENTY-FIVE

Constable Greene opened the first of two double doors to Monk's Pub. When she opened the second set, she was met with the dark-brown tones and yellow-lit atmosphere of the medieval décor. The bar was nestled on the street level of a big Chicago building. If the place was empty, a person could imagine bald monks toiling away at copying scripture for the preservation of Christianity. There was lots of stained glass. Beer steins; Old English fonts on the signs, menus, and pub logo.

Dieter wiped the bar with a rag that should not have been used as often as it was. He slung it on his shoulder and frowned when he laid his eyes on the Constable. The lunch rush hadn't arrived; it was too early and he didn't anticipate seeing Greene.

"Constable. Can I getcha a drink? Bloody Mary? Mimosa? Witches' Brew?" Dieter's thick Chicago accent raked the Constable' ears. She couldn't stand him. She'd wanted to bust him for years, but he somehow kept a good three to four degrees of separation between him and any wrongdoing. His usefulness saved him. Times like these...

"Dieter. I don't want anything to drink. You should know that by now. I wouldn't drink the poison in this place if someone paid me a full year's salary to do so. You know why I am here. You got the alert last night too. We all did."

"Oh, yeah, that black magic shit out in da burbs. Who cares? What da hell does dat have to do wit me?" Dieter placed both hands on the bar he stood behind. "Have a seat."

Constable Greene didn't take a seat on one of the many empty stools at the bar. She stood with her arms crossed. "You are the best guy to go to when someone needs something not sold in the regulated potion shops, Dieter. Notice any strange orders come in lately? Maybe you're getting sloppy in your old age; you allowed a combination of items to be sold in such a short period of time? You didn't think that we would notice?"

"Greeny, I have no idea what da hell you are talkin'

about. No strange orders. Business as usual over here." Dieter shook his head and looked away.

"Dieter. On second thought... I may have a drink of water." Constable Greene pulled out the stool in front of her, sat down, and slammed her wand on the bar top.

"Sure, on da house for you, Constable." Dieter grabbed the hose, pushed the button and, the water shot into a small whiskey glass.

"Again, we have reason to believe that you sold a combination of items that might be used to create dark magic. Dark magic that was used last night and could have murdered someone, Dieter. I know you peddle drugs, temporary highs, cheating spells for students, rare pets from the magical world; you name it, Monk's Pubs best bartender and smuggler has it all. You also rarely turn down a purchase, especially a purchase for a well-to-do client from an affluent suburb. That's a new market for you I would imagine." Constable Greene didn't wait for Dieter to put the water glass on the bar. She ripped it from his hand and took a small sip. Her other hand rested on her wand.

"Alright."

"All right. What, Dieter?"

"We did have a series of orders come in from an anonymous buyer located in one Elburn, Illinois."

"What did this anonymous user buy?"

"I don't have da receipts wit me Greeny. Nothing dat seemed too strange. The odd ingredient or two."

"Odd ingredient or two? Dieter. Come on."

"Merry-mute potion is all I remember off da toppa my head specifically. The other shit was just sensory type stuff. You know, shit teenagers buy for pranks and shit. God's honest truth!" Dieter put his hand over his heart.

Constable Greene took a deep breath. She didn't want to be in Monk's Pub. More and more people were trickling in for lunch. "Address, Dieter. Now."

"Just a PO Box at the local post office. No home address."

"Fine, Dieter. I will work with that. I don't want to be back in here again." She pushed her glass off the bar. It shattered near Dieter's feet. She stood up; she pointed her wand at Dieter and turned toward another worker sweeping the floor. She ripped the broom from the worker's hand and exited through the grimy double doors.

CHAPTER
TWENTY-SIX

Vince did have to pick up his dry cleaning. He had a few shirts and his tux for the wedding in a month. He walked to the small brick building on 5th and Route 38: Mulberry Cleaners. It was a small family-owned establishment with another location on Route 64 in St. Charles, not far from where Vince gave Mac his minivan.

Knowing Debbie was not at work today, Vince thought he could get a few questions answered. Wouldn't hurt. He had picked up clothes before when the other attendant worked at the desk. Sheila was her name, younger, louder, and much kinder than the grizzled Debbie Positano. Vince opened the door and heard the soft ring of a doorbell. It sounded upon entry to alert people in the back that a customer was in.

He flashed a smile. "Good morning, or is it afternoon, yet? Just picking up for Vince O'Malley."

"Almost the afternoon, it's getting there. O'Malley. Great. How are you today?"

"Oh, you know, just a little tired; had a long night last night. Anyway, I never see you in here alone, where is uh, it's Debbie, isn't it? The other lady that works here? She's a riot. Always has the best stories."

"Yeah, she's not in today. I'm sure you heard already about the train incident on Third last night?" Sheila's voice sounded from behind the giant rack of clean and covered shirts.

"Oh, no. What happened?" Vince asked, sounding enthusiastic and empathetic in the same breath.

"Well, Debbie's brother-in-law died on the train last night. Cops are involved. They think it might be a murder. Debbie certainly thinks he was murdered." Sheila stepped out from behind the rack with Vince's clothes. She hung them on the rack next to the front desk while Vince pulled his wallet from his back pocket.

"Oh wow. Who would murder her brother-in-law? That is terrible."

"Yeah, well, her sister and husband have had quite the rough patch lately." Sheila shook her head.

"What do you mean?" Vince opened his mouth in shock at the possible implications.

"I just know they haven't been doing well at all. Debbie's sister's husband always worked late and was never around. We think he may have been involved in some shady investment deals with bigwigs downtown. He could have been offed by them. That's what Debbie tells me," Sheila said.

"So, like an organized crime type hit? Like murdered by a hitman?"

Sheila looked around. She looked outside and then looked at Vince, leaning over the counter.

"I honestly think Debbie is in denial. Wendy, Debbie's sister, probably did it." Sheila whispered.

"Why would she do such a thing?" Vince mirrored her whispered tone.

"Wendy was sleeping with her personal trainer. Her husband found out because she gave her trainer a credit card that Wendy thought was just her own. Exorbitant dinners, gifts, gas money. She bankrolled her personal trainer's life. The husband noticed a change in his credit score and, well, just found the credit card statement. Wendy isn't the brightest bulb. Debbie says she's really taking her husband's death hard. Really hard. Could be guilt. Or overacting. The Positano sisters are a trip, believe me."

"Is she really capable of ordering a hit on her husband?" Vince asked.

"Debbie said he was going to leave her with next-to-nothing due to a prenuptial agreement they signed. This way, there's no divorce and all the money, the house, everything stays with her."

"I'm in shock!"

"Yes, lots of drama in the small town of Geneva. And people tend to leave things in their clothes: they offer up their life stories and drama. You learn a lot about the people of Geneva working here." Sheila smiled.

"Wow, I am in shock. Thanks for letting me know. How much for the clothes again?" Vince's long shot plan worked: community gossip can pay off from time to time. Wendy Rickman could be the person to clear Mac's name. He needed to get back to Wendy's block and keep watch.

CHAPTER

TWENTY-SEVEN

Mac and Millie made their way back to the suburbs in Vince's minivan.

The loud beep of Mac's temporary phone sounded. Millie grabbed it and answered with the speaker enabled.

"Mac. Have some news for you." Vince said. "Please tell me you are halfway to Canada by now."

"We are driving. Not to Canada though." Mac bit his lip.

"Please don't come back here. They will be waiting for you; they're expecting you to return. Moron. Anyway, I have some interesting news. Wendy Rickman and Peter Rickman had some major marital issues and people around town think she may have called in a hit on him. She certainly has the purse to do something like that."

"Yes, but how Vince? How did the hitman kill him? He was bleeding from his ear and it looked like something hard hit him. Would hitting the floor super hard cause that?" Mac said.

"He could have hit his head on the seats on the way down. There are several poisons that cause bleeding from the ears, too. He could have been poisoned. It was a bachelor party; it was probably at a rowdy bar where someone could have dropped poison into his drink." Vince's voice sounded worse through the cheap phone as time went on.

"Ugh. I guess it's something to investigate. Can you get to Wendy to question her?"

"I tried, but Jackson already got to her and warned them about me. The sister wouldn't let me in and told me I should bring your ass in. Please tell me you aren't heading back here."

Mac looked at Millie. They both opened their eyes wide. The Positano sister blocked Vince from talking to Wendy—it could be something. Could be nothing. Still.

"We will stay away, Vince." Mac lied. He didn't want to stress his brother out further.

"I'll stake out the Rickman's block. If they move, I

will let you know. Stay put and let me do my job. Ah shit. Jackson's rolling up next to me. I gotta go." Vince ended the call.

Millie closed the flip phone. "Well, well, well, the Positano sisters could be the dark magic users who killed Peter. Vince didn't say what marital issues, though."

"I guess it doesn't matter. There's a ton of money involved. If they were going to get a divorce, Wendy could be protecting her stake in the fortune. We also have Sherry Dachowitz as well, who was obsessed with Peter. At least we have some leads here."

"True. Where we are headed; The Positano mansion in Elburn? I remember there being some strange stories about that place from when I was a kid." Millie said.

"What stories? Is it legit haunted like the Wanderer is?"

"Not haunted. Just bizarre. The parents were eccentric and came from old money. Multi-generational wealth. The mother was rumored to have murdered their dad: just plugged in an appliance and threw it in the pool when the dad was swimming."

"Whoa. What?!?"

"Yes, and the mom was also obsessed with dolls and mannequins—so much so, that she displayed them in the windows. Naturally, you can guess how creepy that looked to everyone who drove past."

"Are you sure these aren't just some crazy, local scary stories?"

"I do remember going past there as a teenager and seeing the mannequins in the window. So that part is at least true." Millie said.

"We have got to see this place; even with Wendy and Debbie not at home. Checking the place out might be beneficial."

"Are we just going to break in or something? I can't remember if the mom is still alive."

"Let's just get there and see what happens! Gotta take action Millie! Off to the creepy house of mannequins and death we go!" Mac pumped his fist.

CHAPTER
TWENTY-EIGHT

"Vince, you really should just go home." Detective Jackson said though his rolled down drivers window outside of Mulberry's Dry cleaners.

"What the hell, am I under house arrest? I just picked up my dry-cleaning, Jackson. No crime there. No meddling."

"Where's your car, Vince?"

"What, a guy can't walk?" Vince scrunched his face up like Bob DeNiro in any number of mob flicks.

"You live on the east side of the river; that's a substantial hike from here, Vince. Come on, hop in and I'll drive you home."

"Get the hell outta here. I want to walk."

"Vince. Debbie Positano called and said you came

to Wendy's door. Just get in the car and let me drive you home."

Vince had had enough. "Jackson. I swear, if you don't just leave me the fuck alone, you'll have to find a new partner and a new face."

Detective Jackson shook his head. Vince walked away from the unmarked squad car.

"It would be in your best interest to bring your brother in. Call him, Vince!"

"Oh, now you want my help, superstar Detective? Go away!" Vince yelled.

Vince didn't really want to lug all his dry cleaning around while trying to get back to Wendy's house. He needed to get off Route 38. There was too much exposure. He needed to return to the Rickman's house and talk to Wendy; grill her and extract a confession. His brother liked the sleuthing part. Vince liked the interrogation part.

He walked down Fourth Street and away from the main drag; he kept an eye out for Jackson's squad. There was nothing in sight. After he dumped his dry cleaning in some bushes in front of someone's house, he turned around and looked toward Route 38. He was going to have to cross it to get back to Fulton and the Rickman house. He jogged toward the main street—and then saw an orange Bronco turn onto Route 38.

The same car that was parked in the Rickman's driveway.

Wendy and Debbie were on the move: headed east down Route 38.

Vince pulled his phone out. He had friends in the force who would help him, despite him being off the case.

"Hello, Vincey, how's your time off?"

"Danny, I don't need your shit right now. Your squad close?"

"Yeah, why? I'm at the new Dinkin Donuts."

"Seriously, of all places. A donut shop!"

"Yes, I am hungry and needed more coffee, Vince. You big jerk!"

"Danny, there is an orange Ford Bronco heading east on 38 right now. Heading towards you. I need to you tail it. It's a lead I am working for this train debacle."

"Yeah. Alright. On it."

Vince could hear shuffling in his ear. A door opening. Some wind.

"I see it. It's at the 25 light just down the hill." Officer Danny said. "I'm on pursuit."

"Danny, do not engage or anything. Just follow that Bronco! I'm on the way!"

"Ha! This is cool: another famous Bronco chase!"

Danny laughed.

Vince just ended the call. He couldn't handle the amount of crap this day was bringing him. He ran as hard as he could down Route 38. The exertion made him feel out of shape and could feel his belly jiggle. Still, he powered through. He had no choice.

CHAPTER
TWENTY-NINE

Officer Danny Zambrano hopped in his black squad car with a blue Geneva PD splash on the side doors. He didn't call anything in. The chatter of the police radio spouted the usual codes and checks. He pulled out of the Dinkin' Donuts lot and looked down the hill. The Bronco took a right and headed south down Route 25.

He drove the squad to the light, and it turned green right when he needed it most. His stomach growled. Stupid Vince and his hunches. Danny really wanted some donuts.

The orange Bronco stuck out like a sore thumb. Easy to spot, track, and follow. Hopefully, it won't be a long drive. He could be back at the Dinks in no time.

He noticed the Bronco pull off 25 and into the

Fabyan Windmill lot. A leisurely stroll on a chilly day? Why the windmill? Danny pulled his squad to the side of the road. The windmill did look impressive. The gray and brown historic Dutch windmill stood sixty-eight feet in the air with four massive blades proudly catching the wind on the east bank of the Fox River.

Two women exited the Bronco. One blonde, the other brunette. The brunette held a picnic basket in her hand.

The blonde woman walked slowly and held a tissue box in her left hand.

Danny called Vince.

"Hel—hello." Vince panted in Danny's ear.

"The Bronco stopped at Fabyan Windmill. It's not open today but looks like they may just have a picnic."

"Good, stay—stay there. I am near... well, getting close to the Hennington bridge. Be there soon. Keep an eye on them for me will ya?"

"Yep. Got it. See you soon."

Constable Greene finally had what she needed—enough to win the day. She flew over 272 Witchhazel's gate and landed near the door.

The Paderson family would help her track down Millie.

She wouldn't give them a choice. She just flew at very high speeds from downtown to Elburn and now to Geneva. The Constable's hunger, fatigue, and overall demeanor did little to create a welcoming and warm vibe to those she interacted with. She pounded on the green front door.

The door opened quickly. A white-haired man in a blue active shirt stood in the doorframe.

"You must be Hank. I need to speak with your daughter. Was hoping you could help me. I believe she may be in grave danger."

CHAPTER
THIRTY

Mac and Millie drove down Interstate 88. Millie's phone rang.

"Millie Paderson, don't be alarmed—it's me Constable Greene. You aren't in trouble. Your fiancé isn't in trouble and your parents certainly aren't."

Millie's stomach dropped. "You're at my parents' house? What's going on?"

"I have reason to believe the Positano family of Elburn used the dark magic that you were worried about. I now know it's not you two. You can relax. I think it would be best if we worked together, as your parents tell me you are now quite the detective yourself." Constable Greene's voice sounded strong. Confident. But impatient.

"Okay, um. Yes. Sorry, just gathering my thoughts here, um, yes. Can I talk to my dad?"

"Millie, everything's fine. The Constable is here to help." Hank said.

"Millie, let's just work together here."

Mac nodded to Millie.

"We're actually on the way to the Positano house now, but it looks like we don't have to go that far. Mac, just get off at Farnsworth. We don't need to go all the way to 47." Millie pointed to an exit marked by a big retail outlet mall.

"Yes, we believe the Positanos over the past few weeks bought certain items that could be combined and used as forbidden potion. It's been known to cause bleeding from the facial orifices like the ears and nose. The poison is called Hear-No-Evil."

"Yes, I remember from Magic History class. It was developed because of the Salem Witch Trials. But why that potion? Why not just use regular arsenic; why go to such lengths to make a highly volatile potion that killed more people than silenced them?" Millie asked.

"Lots of questions that still need answers. I checked the Positano house. No one was there, even though it looked like people were in the windows—they were all either dolls or mannequins. Very strange. I had my junior constables run a check on the Positano family and found an interesting connection to Peter Rickman."

"Her sister was Peter's wife."

"Exactly. We sent owls to observe the Rickman house in Geneva. They've since left the house and were tracked to Fabyan Windmill on Route 25. The sisters appear to be having a picnic together. Meet me there, but just observe. Don't engage with them and park a block or so away. What car are you in?"

"A blue minivan. Sounds good. See you soon." Millie ended the call. She felt better being allied with the Constable rather than against her.

"Are we allies with the evil Constabulary now?" Mac asked.

"The day gets stranger and stranger. Let's get to the windmill."

CHAPTER
THIRTY-ONE

Vince couldn't keep running. He jogged at this point, and the jog was slow and half-hearted. More like a limping half-step. He made it to Route 25 and looked at the hill he would have to climb. He put his hands on his knees. Sweat dripped onto the sidewalk. The hill didn't seem appealing and he was starting to feel a slight pain in his chest. It just was not worth it. Vince fished for his phone in his pocket. Danny could help.

"Vincey, nothing much happening here. They are just setting up their little picnic on a chilly, gloomy day in early May. Doesn't make much sense. I'm really hungry for some Dinkins. Damn you, Vince." Danny joked.

"Okay, well, that seems like they aren't going

anywhere anytime soon. Please just come pick me up so I can get another shot at talking to Wendy." Vince panted.

"Gotta hit the gym more often, Vincey."

"Says the guy who eats donuts every day. I don't want to run anymore. I'm at the corner of 38 and 25. Come get me."

Mac and Millie parked about 200 yards away from the turn-off to the Fabyan Windmill parking lot. Before they could exit the vehicle, Constable Greene opened the driver side door for Mac.

"Wow, what service. Mac O'Malley." Mac exited the vehicle and a familiar pain shot up the nerves in his leg. Millie's temporary cure apparently had started to run out.

"Constable Greene. Went to school with your fiancé. Glad we are on the same team; you should have come to me earlier."

"We didn't want to be blamed for the dark magic use. We needed to get away from the reg authorities as well." Millie walked over to the driver side of the van and the road bordered by trees and, just beyond, the river.

"Were you able to find any actual evidence around the Positano house in Elburn?" Mac asked.

"No. We only have the registry that connects the Positano magic user family and a black-market magic dealer sending banned materials to a PO Box in Elburn. That's why we're here now. We could just ask them a few things and see if we can find anything else out." Constable Greene pulled out a wand and balanced it in her palm.

"My wand!" Millie felt a jolt of excitement seeing her wand again.

"Nice work sending me on a wild wand chase." Constable Greene cracked a smile.

"Pretty impressive tracking my wand. Not exactly legal, is it?" Millie secured her wand.

"It's a grey area."

Mac's phone buzzed in his pocket. Vince.

"Mac!" his voice burst from the speaker for all to hear.

"Any updates for us?" Mac asked.

"Yes, we're following Wendy and Debbie. Debbie's co-worker fed me some interesting gossip. She thinks that Wendy wanted her husband dead. She was banging her personal trainer and Peter found out. They signed a prenup and she stands to lose big-time in the divorce." Vince sounded tired.

"Wait, where are the sisters now?"

"Fabyan Windmill of all places. Apparently having a picnic. Anyway, I'm going to see if I can talk to Wendy and get some answers. Danny picked me up in his squad. Will keep you updated. Please keep the van in one piece. Out."

"Shit! Vince is on his way down Route 25 now in a GPD SUV. He won't understand all this magical craziness. Isn't that bad? Don't you guys like to keep things separate?" Mac asked. His leg hurt. *A lot*. Again.

"I will take care of it. I'll have the Junior Constables run interference. It'll buy us some time."

"Also, the Fabyan Windmill. Interesting place. I think I saw a picture of Peter and Wendy at the windmill in one of the pictures in his office. This place must have some historical meaning for her. Let's get moving!" Mac grabbed the cane from the backseat of the van.

CHAPTER
THIRTY-TWO

Millie, the Constable, and Mac—public enemy #1—made their way along the treelined road and to the open field in front of the Dutch windmill. They stopped near an Orange Bronco in the parking lot. The only evidence of the sisterly picnic was an empty picnic basket and a blanket on the ground about fifty yards away from the front of the windmill.

The wind gusted and the large blades creaked in motion.

"Where are they?" Mac asked.

Constable Greene examined a piece of parchment pulled from her back pocket. "The owls saw them go into the windmill."

"The old paper told you that?"

"You bet." Constable Greene readied her wand in her right hand and walked towards the windmill.

Millie readied her wand as well and followed Greene along the grass path to the windmill.

Mac pointed his cane, mimicking the two witches, and began to walk. He then realized he *did* need the cane to walk and followed the ladies.

Constable Greene stopped at the blanket and picnic basket. She knelt to examine the basket's contents: empty brown bottles and a picture. "Is this the picture you described, Mac?"

Mac hobbled over as fast as his cane and functional leg could take him. "Yes, that is exactly the picture."

"I saw that picture too."

"What does that mean? Could just be something sentimental. Her husband just died." Millie said.

"The brown bottles—these are the ingredients." Constable Greene waved her hands up at a tree. "They must be doing something in the windmill with these materials."

Two owls swooped down and over to the windmill. They were careful not to hit the blades and flew around the structure, looking through small windows. There were eight windows at various heights on the windmill. The two owls finally settled down and perched on a window in the middle-center of the building.

"That's where they are. Come on. We must get in there." Constable Greene sprinted toward the door of the windmill.

Danny picked up Vince with the stipulation of a quick donut and coffee run to Dinkin. That took way more time than Vince wanted it to take.

"Finally. Christ. What is wrong with you?" Vince raged.

The smell of coffee did little to calm him.

"Relax. Those two chicks were just chilling at the park." Danny bit into his donut.

Danny pulled out of Dink's lot and turned left onto Rt. 38, making his way down the hill to the light at 25. He turned left and he and Vince made their way up another hill. The glaciers that carved the Fox River left a few rolling hills in the otherwise flat geography of The Prairie State.

Danny floored the gas pedal at Vince's request when suddenly the pedal gave way.

"Danny, what the hell is going on? We need to get back to the windmill!" Vince shook his head.

"I don't know; the pedal just gave way. I'm not getting any resistance, no gas, nothing!" Danny kept pounding on the gas pedal.

"Of all the damn times, on a fricking hill!" Vince looked out the back window. Luckily there were no cars behind them.

Danny hit the brakes and the SUV jolted to a stop. Then turned to block the road; the car rolled until half was in the opposite lane.

"What the hell is going on? I didn't turn the car!" Danny's donut fell onto his lap. Crumbs showered all over his shirt and pants.

"Looks like we are walking then." Vince reached for the car door and pulled the latch. Locked. It didn't budge. "Danny, unlock the doors."

"I'm trying! Nothing's working!"

"Great. Just great. What a damn day." Vince hit the console very hard with a balled-up hammer fist.

"I'll call for help." Danny grabbed the radio receiver. Within milliseconds, the car turned off completely. They were just stuck on a hill, blocking the road.

"What about our cell phones?" Vince pulled out his phone.

Danny shook his head. "Mine's dead."

"Shit. Mine too."

CHAPTER
THIRTY-THREE

Millie sprinted and nearly surpassed Constable Greene. She slowed her pace to match Greene's. There was a small door at the base of the windmill; Millie thought she may have to crouch to get in. Greene took a position to the left of the door and Millie on the right. They both readied their wands in preparation for what they might face from the witches within.

Constable Greene raised her index finger to signal quiet. She then tapped the wand to her ear and then pointed it at Millie's. Millie's ear felt cold then quickly shifted to warm.

The whoosh of the gentle wind. Birds chirping. The hoot of the Constabulary's owl above. Mac shuffled behind them and drove his cane into the earth. Every sound louder. More pronounced.

Voices from within the windmill.

"This will help you get through this, but it could do irreparable damage." An older female's voice maybe early 60s, was loud in Millie's ear.

"Just... just do it. We've made it this far." Another female voice spoke; it sounded similar in age.

Debbie and Wendy.

"Are you sure? There were good memories too, Wendy."

"It's just too much." Wendy's voice trembled. "Too much."

"All you have to do is drink it." Debbie's older, raspier voice sounded from within.

Millie looked at Constable Greene, who nodded. Constable Greene gripped the door handle.

She opened the door a crack. She didn't see anyone in her line of sight—just an empty front hall and a spiral stairwell. The sisters conversed a floor or two above them. Constable Greene moved into the windmill. Millie followed close behind.

"He was very sweet at first. Very connected. We were connected. Then life...time..there just wasn't enough fight in us to keep together. He brought me up here once; made a really bad joke about me being the wind beneath his wings. Then he got down on one knee." Wendy shared.

"I know the story, Wendy. We should go. Just take this and I promise, I'll take care of everything else. You won't have to worry anymore. I'm sorry it happened like this." Debbie said.

"We should never have tried to pull this shit, Debbie! We should've let things play out. You... we..." Wendy cried.

"Wendy, I don't know how many times I can say that I'm sorry. This will help. This will help you move on."

"Just give it to me."

MAC DIDN'T KNOW if he should follow Millie or not. He heeded the warning Millie gave him to be quiet, but she didn't say to stay back. He pushed his cane into the grass and kept moving forward to the door. Suddenly, Millie's hand sprouted from behind the door and shooed him away.

Mac sighed. His leg felt more sore than usual. He paced back and forth; he looked up at the owls. They stared down at him like he was their prey.

Mac glared back and stuck his tongue out at them

for good measure. The owls just rotated their crazy heads and hooted.

"Step away from the windmill, Officer O'Malley!" A familiar voice spoke from behind Mac.

"Okay, okay. I don't like windmills anyway. I always feel like I'm going to get whacked by the blades." Mac turned around.

Sherry Dachowitz, Peter's lovelorn assistant, pointed a hunter's shotgun at Mac. Mac put his hands and cane up.

"I need to settle this. You need to get down on the grass now." Sherry's voice didn't quiver. Didn't shake. Her calm alarmed Mac.

"I could use a snooze. It's totally fine. I'm not sure you want to go in there right now, though. Tell me, Sherry, what exactly are you doing here?" Mac knelt with his cane still planted firmly into the soil.

Sherry fired a shot at the ground in front of Mac. Dirt and grass exploded in his face. Mac fell to the ground. The loud shot cracked off the windmill and out into the field like a crash of thunder.

CHAPTER
THIRTY-FOUR

Millie and the Constable's stealthy approach failed. The shotgun's loud blast scared Millie. Her heart leapt into her throat and then sank as she burst through the door to see if Mac was okay. She felt a sudden jolt backwards into the windmill. Constable Greene pulled her back and shut the door.

"Get down!" Greene shouted.

A burst of pellets blew through the door. Wooden shards and slivers filled the dusty air of the windmill's interior.

Millie's ear hurt from the hearing spell combined with the loud shots.

Constable Greene heard the barrel drop. The shooter stopped to reload the gun.

"Get upstairs. Higher ground will be to our advantage and we need to stop Wendy before she drinks that potion. Go."

Millie rolled to the stairwell and sprinted up the spiral steps. The swirling movement gave her stomach a creeping sickness. She looked up and there was a floor above, but it was near the top of the windmill. With so many stairs left, Millie climbed as fast as she could—partly in thanks to her conditioning in softball on Augie's campus. There were lots of hills, lots of stairs to climb, lots of up and down, but it built the strength in her legs.

The first red streak bounced off of a railing. The second whizzed past her arm.

Wendy and Debbie hurled dueling magic at her from above.

Millie twirled her wand, and a yellow umbrella of light covered her ascent. She needed to hold the wand up and concentrate to keep the umbrella shield active.

Constable Greene peppered the upper swirl of the staircase with her green dueling magic sparks. They were rapid fire and incessant.

"Keep climbing with the shield and I will be right behind you. Let's keep going Millie!" Constable Greene called.

"What about the shooter below us?"

. . .

Mac tasted the grass. It brought back memories of football in his neighborhood when he and the other kids used to ruin each other's pre-winter lawns by playing tackle football.

He dismissed his nostalgia quickly and observed as Sherry secured the barrel back into place. She'd loaded two more shots into the dual shotgun.

And then she blew a hole through the windmill door.

Mac took a deep breath. The despair and rage he felt from Millie's possible death blinded him.

Damn his bum leg.

He pulled himself to his feet and gripped his cane; he rushed Sherry from behind.

She turned around and aimed at his chest.

CHAPTER
THIRTY-FIVE

Millie and Constable Greene kept moving up the spiral steps. Orange and red casts meant to paralyze and disarm the good witches below whizzed and sparkled all around them.

"They're trapped up there. We have the advantage. Let's keep going!" Constable Greene urged Millie upward. They had a quarter of the spiral staircase left to climb.

"We're almost there. I won't be able to shield us both when we get up there: the floor is built around the stairwell. We'll be exposed."

"The owls! I'll call the owls into distract. We need to make sure we get everything they have up there intact. I would say we can blow the floor out from underneath them, but...yeah, maybe too extreme."

Greene laughed. She enjoyed the thrill of bewitched combat.

"Yes, definitely too extreme." Millie's shoulder ached from holding up the magical umbrella shield.

"What? We could easily catch them as they fell!" Greene laughed.

"I'm not feeling anymore hits on the shield."

Millie and Greene's strategic exchange distracted them. The death spells from above ceased.

"You're right. They stopped. Wendy! Debbie! Put your wands down and come down the steps with your hands up!"

The only response was silence, except for the creaking wood floorboards. They were still up there.

"What are they doing?" Millie asked.

MAC THREW the cane like a javelin. Sherry pulled the shotgun up—but still fired. She darted to the side of the projectile, but Mac kept moving. Engaging his inner Butkus, he raced towards Sherry, hitting her in the rib cage with his shoulder. She dropped the shot gun and Mac pinned her.

"Shotgun Sherry, you need to relax!"

"No! No! Nooooo! There she is! Let me kill her! She did it! She murdered him!"

"There's no one out here."

"Look up, idiot! Let me end this!" Sherry screamed.

Mac looked up and saw a woman climbing down and clinging to one of the Fabyan Windmill's thirty-foot blades. She was still very high up, about fifty feet in the air, but she just needed to reach the outer balcony platform—which was about twenty feet up from the ground.

Mac didn't want to let Sherry go. He kept her pinned to the ground.

"Millie! Constable! Anyone! One of them is on the blade! Hello? Help!"

Constable Greene kicked the damaged door down and ran to Mac and Sherry.

"Where's Millie?! Is she okay?"

"She's fine. Debbie! Get down from there now, or I'll make this very unpleasant for you!" Constable Greene pointed the wand at Debbie Positano, who continued to make her way down the blade. There was no wind to propel the blades and she'd almost reached the balcony above.

Constable Greene aimed to change that. A propulsion spell would do the trick.

Debbie neared the balcony. Surprisingly nimble and quick, Debbie ignored the Constable's warnings.

"Propulso!" Constable Greene aimed her wand and

a beam of green magic spiraled forth.

Mac saw leaves on the ground kick up; he felt his hair move. A blast of air traveled from Greene's wand to the blades of the windmill.

Debbie let go of the blade just before the wind spell jolted the old blades into motion. She hit the balcony hard.

"Don't you dare move!" Constable Greene yelled. She made her way back into the windmill and headed toward the balcony.

"Caw! Caw! Caw! Caw!" A cacophony of bird calls sounded from all the trees in the park and across the river. Mac tried his best to keep Sherry pinned.

"What the hell is happening?" Mac looked up.

A vast murder of crows flew toward the windmill from all directions. Hitchcock's *Birds* couldn't compare to this spectacle. An overcast dim covered the land Mac and Sherry lay on as the murder of crows swirled around the windmill. Mac put his head down next to Sherry's. It was an awkward position but was the safest now—the crows began to peck at his back and neck.

The cawing and pecking became so overwhelming. All Mac and Sherry could do was scream.

"AHHHHHH!!!!"

Mac felt blood trickle down his neck.

CHAPTER
THIRTY-SIX

Millie reached the top of the windmill where the turbine connected to the blades. The windows revealed thousands of crows circling the area. Millie kept her wand at the ready should the crows penetrate the windmill.

"They won't come in." A sickly voice resounded from next to the turbine.

Millie looked up and around with wand pointed. "How can you be so sure?"

"I know my sister; she's just using them to escape. She's long gone by now."

The constant caw, flaps, and hits to the windmill dissipated. The murder of crows flew away.

"And you are?" Millie knew but wanted confirmation.

"I am Wendy. I'm Wendy...though I might not remember in a few seconds." Wendy dangled a brown, corked topped bottle at Millie from her seated position in the corner.

"Wendy, if that's what I think it is, you could possibly die or suffer brain damage. You could be paralyzed." Millie connected the clues from the hearing spell, the picnic basket, and Constable Greene's warnings.

"It wasn't supposed to happen this way. We were supposed to be happy. She was supposed to just help him forget." Wendy kept talking.

"Help who forget?" Millie asked.

"My soon-to-be ex-husband. I cheated on him." Wendy rubbed her eyes. Millie noted how defeated she looked. Her frown, the lines in her forehead; the way her shoulders slumped.

"What did Debbie say she would do for you?" Millie knelt next to Wendy within grabbing distance of the bottle she held.

"She said she would just make him forget about the affair; that it would be possible to just reset and get back to normal."

"I don't know how to help you, Wendy, but your sister lied. She couldn't do the things she said. Magic doesn't work like that; it can't change fates or fortunes, and especially feelings. I am so sorry, but your sister misled you." Millie inched a bit closer.

Constable Greene emerged from the spiral staircase. "Millie's right. Your sister tried to concoct a Hear-No-Evil potion. It's a form of dark magic used to silence and mess with people's senses and cognitive function; it was created during periods where witch hunts and persecution were commonplace. It caused Peter to hemorrhage blood from his ear and killed him. What you are holding won't make you forget, Wendy. It is a form of Dark Magic, and it will kill you."

Wendy held the bottle close to her eyes and examined it.

Greene stepped forward. Millie put her hand up and shot the aggressive Constable a look to stand down.

"Wendy, you can turn this around. You can give Peter justice and do right by him. We just need you to give us that bottle." Millie held out her hand.

Wendy froze. She took a deep breath and handed Millie the bottle.

Millie grabbed the bottle and Constable Greene rushed over to secure Wendy in handcuffs.

CHAPTER
THIRTY-SEVEN

Mac and Millie walked down Third Street on their way to the Tiny Wanderer to meet with Edith and finalize details of the wedding ceremony. They were delighted to get married on the lawn of the Wanderer.

"What a wild time. I'm really glad we were able to figure that mess out. Thank you again for your help." Mac kissed Millie on the cheek.

"Me too. I am glad we convinced Greene to stand down and let Vince and Jackson have Wendy. She is now hell bent on finding Debbie. Debbie presents a threat the magical world hasn't dealt with in a long time: a possible full-blown sorceress situation." Millie grabbed Mac's hand.

"Greene and her junior constables were slick putting traces of Warfarin into Peter's flask after the fact. We got lucky there, even if it's a bit of a stretch that it could cause that much bleeding. There's a precedent, though. With Wendy's full cooperation and confession, this can officially be put to bed. Except, I am concerned about the toxicology report. Can Greene fix those?"

"Yes, Wendy knows the implications of mixing the magical and real world. Believe me, she knows the human justice system is less punishing than the magical world. We did make a deal with Greene though: she may call upon us to find Debbie one day and we'll have to help. And yes, the report will be taken care of, too. The magical world stays hidden for a reason, my dear. How is the Vince and Jackson situation?" Millie shook her head.

"Not a proponent of doctoring evidence and tampering with investigations, but whatevs. Jackson did find out the bachelor party itinerary from Peter's brother. Debbie with Wendy's key entered Peter's downtown condo on the night of the bachelor party before they all came back for the stripper show apparently. That was when Debbie dosed his flask with the potion that killed him. So, he gets to be the hero too. Vince is back at work. He was focused on what happened to Danny's car and their phones but dropped it when Wendy turned herself in. We are lucky." Mac squeezed her hand.

The couple stopped in front of their favorite place on Third Street. The vibrant green grass led to the traditional porch, white siding, black shutters, and lush flower boxes of its welcoming façade. The venerable, historic, and cherished thirty-six room retail mansion, The Tiny Wanderer, where they would soon be saying *I Do*.

"Things were looking grim there for a minute." Millie put her head on Mac's shoulder.

"Yes, things were looking very grim, but now things are looking great for an eternity. You are the person I get to spend forever with and that's all I will ever need."

"Yeah, yeah, yeah you need me *and* murders to solve." Millie laughed.

"Well, maybe it's a combination with a slight bias towards murder-mystery solving."

"I TOTALLY GET IT. Me too. I don't even know why I like you anymore! Let's just cancel this wedding thing." Millie said.

Mac laughed out loud. "Never, Future Mrs. O'Malley. We are doing this!"

Mac and Millie shared a hard-earned laugh and a kiss.

THE MAC AND MILLIE MYSTERY SERIES

Book 1: The Christmas Walk Caper

Book 2: The Valentine Dine or Die

Book 3: The Swedish Days Swindle

Book 4: Festival of the Vine

Book 5: Raftery's Ghost

Book 6: This book... duh

THE TANNENBAUM TAILORS SERIES

Book 1: The Secret Snowball

Book 2: The Brethren of the Saints

Book 3: A Capitol Abduction

CHRONICLES OF THE ORDER SERIES

Prequel: The Ancient Order

Book 1: The Elixir

Book 2: The Castle

Book 3: Phantom of the Catacombs

Book 4: The Horde

"Millie has requested that I formally query you for your opinion of this crazy adventure in the form of a book review. So please leave a review of *"Murder on Geneva Express."* We thank you very much.

- Mac, non-writer and former Chicago cop

Copyright © 2023 by JB Michaels

All rights reserved.

No part of this book may be reproduced in any form or by any electronic or mechanical means, including information storage and retrieval systems, without written permission from the author, except for the use of brief quotations in a book review.

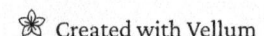

❀ Created with Vellum

ABOUT THE AUTHOR

JB Michaels is a USA Today Bestselling Author and Amazon Bestselling Author. His work has won seven Literary Achievement Awards over the span of his career starting with the wondrous and imaginative Tannenbaum Tailors series to the dark and thrilling Chronicles of the Order series. JB's books have been read around the world, reached #1 in multiple categories, and continue to delight readers both young and old alike.

Made in the USA
Monee, IL
28 October 2023